The Boy :
who walkei

Nicholas Cross came to live in Spain following a period of service in the army, and a
degree course in anthropology.

Together with his father, and their dogs,
cats and geese, he works a small holding
near the tiny village of Archez, in the valley
of the Rio Agarrobo, in the shadow of the
great Sierra Almijira.

Nicholas Cross

The Boy and the Dog
who walked to the Moon

Flyways

Illustrations by Georgina McBain

First published in 2000 by Flyways, an imprint of Floris Books

British Library CIP Data available

ISBN 0-86315-314-3

Printed in Great Britain
by Cromwell Press, Trowbridge

In memory of Gabri

Contents

Chapter One

Don Alfonso de Albaricoque y Dos Limones

In a time so long ago that it might have been yesterday, in the splendidly mysterious city of Granada, there lived a young orphan boy called Tomás. For most of his life, or as much of it as he could remember, Tomás had worked at the inn of Fat Francisco and his large, jolly wife, Carmen. The inn, La Peña, lay just inside the great city walls on the busy main road that ran to the north, and provided good food and a comfortable bed for the night for the many *muleros* who travelled the wild sierras and burning plains.

Every day, just before the sun rose over the snowcapped peaks of the Sierra Nevada, Tomás was hard at work, sweeping out the inn, cleaning the tables and making ready for the early customers. When Francisco and Carmen finally arrived, Tomás was able to gather together his lunch of bread and goat's cheese and drive Fat Francisco's goats out of the city and on to the slopes of the great sierra.

In the evening, once the goats had been settled in their pen, Tomás had to work in the kitchen, where Carmen heaved and spluttered over her cooking pots. Then, only after the last plate had been cleaned and the last knife put away, could Tomás creep off to the tiny outhouse, next to the goat pen, where he slept.

For Tomás the days were long and the work hard. Though Francisco and Carmen treated him well, the boy felt deep down inside that there must be more to life than this daily toil, but had no idea what. Every night, as he lay on his bed of straw listening to the goats moving about in their pen, he would look up through his little window and watch the moon as it shone in the sky. Tomás felt sometimes that the moon was trying to speak to him and, just before he drifted off to sleep, he would smile up at the beautiful, silent face and feel contented. The Moon has always been able to talk to her special creatures, but they have to know how to listen first.

One fine day, Tomás led Fat Francisco's goats out on to the Sierra Nevada, to where the tall pine trees grew. He was taking them to a spot further away from the city than normal to try and find fresh grazing. It was autumn and the rains had not yet come to bring back the sweet grass.

The sun was high in the sky and shining fiercely down on to the dry, red earth. Tomás sat down in the shade of some trees to eat his meal. As he did so, he happened to notice a thin, brown dog hobbling towards him on three good legs. The fourth, a front one, the dog held up, limp, beneath his chest. Tomás watched as the dog approached to within two paces and sat down facing him, panting from his hot walk, his pink tongue hanging out from the side of his mouth.

"Can you spare me some water?" the dog asked thirstily.

Tomás was amazed and rubbed his eyes to make sure that he had not fallen asleep. He had never heard a dog speak before.

"Did you hear me, boy?" the dog asked crossly. "I am very thirsty. I have come a long way in this heat and only ask that you give me a little of your water."

"Y...y...you can speak." Tomás managed to say.

"Of course I can speak. You speak, don't you?"

"Yes, but I'm a boy. You're a dog and dogs only bark."

The dog howled an annoyed howl. "Dogs only bark, young man, because people are too stupid to listen to them," he replied tartly. "Now, are you going to offer me a little of your water? While you're about it, a morsel from that delicious loaf that you have before you would certainly ease my hunger."

Tomás smiled and, without saying another

word, removed his hat and filled it to the brim from his water bottle. The dog drank thirstily until the water had gone. When he had finished he looked up as Tomás took out his round loaf of bread and broke it in two, offering half to the dog, who took it and, in a casual sort of way, ate it.

"Do you want some cheese?" Tomás asked politely.

The dog sighed. "Dear friend," he murmured, "a little of your goat's cheese would be most acceptable."

Tomás took out his cheese, cut it into two equal portions and gave one to the dog who sighed and lay down at Tomás' feet to eat it.

"How did you learn to talk like people?" Tomás asked once the dog had made himself comfortable.

"The same way that you did," came the reply.

"But ..." Tomás began.

"But I'm a dog. I know, I know. I'll have you know, young man, that all dogs can speak; some more eloquently than others it's true, but then people, in my experience, are the same." The dog continued, "You know cats can talk too, though as a general rule they don't choose to because, I suppose, that's the way it is with cats. Donkeys and mules are quite interesting, but you tend to find that goats and sheep can only talk about family, which most of us find a bit boring, especially if you don't happen to be related to any of them."

14

"You mean to say that these goats can talk?" Tomás asked in surprise, pointing towards the flock that was quietly grazing some distance away.

"Certainly."

"What happened to your leg?" Tomás asked, changing the subject.

The dog howled an exasperated howl. "Questions, questions, all the time questions," he complained.

"Well, be fair," Tomás appealed, "what am I to do when a dog comes hobbling up to me demanding to be fed and watered? You've got to admit that it's a bit of a surprise."

The dog stretched out in the warm afternoon sun. His belly full, he felt that he could tell the boy about himself. "You were asking about my leg?" he began. "Well, a long time ago, when I was a youngster, I was kept on a chain in the yard of a man who made barrels for the wine trade."

"A cooper?" Tomás interrupted.

"Yes, boy, a cooper," the dog continued. "One day I was sitting, as we dogs do, watching the antics of the humans as they loaded the huge barrels on to wagons using ropes and levers to help them when, unluckily, a rope snapped and a barrel came rolling towards me. You see, I was chained and couldn't run away so all I could do was to press myself against the wall and await my fate. Somehow the barrel missed me, but ran over my poor left leg, crushing it entirely.

15

"Of course, after the accident, I was precious little use as a guard dog so the cooper threw me out and I have been on the road ever since. What about you?"

Tomás told the dog as much as he could about himself — the life he led; being an orphan and having no family; how he had been brought up by the monks and put to work as soon as he was able for Fat Francisco and his wife.

"You and me are about the same then, Tomás," the dog observed. "We are both looking for something. Perhaps we would be better looking together?"

This sounded a bit strange to Tomás. "What are you doing, dog?" he asked. "Where are you going? I don't even know what to call you. I can't very well keep calling you Dog, can I?"

The dog sat up and scratched himself before replying. "My name, young man, is Don Alfonso de Albaricoque y Dos Limones, at your service, and I am walking to the Moon."

Tomás shook his head, for he could hardly believe what he was hearing. "The Moon?" he asked. "The Moon up there?" he added, pointing to the sky.

"The very same. I certainly know of no other, do you?"

The boy was so amazed by what Don Alfonso told him that he had quite lost track of his goats who, by this time, were ambling all over the slope, eating wherever they chose. "Well no," he agreed, "but how can you walk to the Moon? After all, we are here," he thumped the ground with his fist, "and the Moon is up there. Besides, who would want to walk to the Moon anyway? It seems like a very silly idea to me."

"Just listen to me," Don Alfonso told him. "I will try and explain.

"A long time ago, (we dogs measure these things differently from you), but not long after the cooper had thrown me out following my accident, I happened to meet a wise, white sheepdog called Gabri. I considered myself to be very lucky at the time to have met such a dog as Gabri because he had 'the Mark' on him."

"The Mark?" Tomás asked.

"Questions, questions," Don Alfonso replied irritably. "Why can't you humans just accept what *is* and what is not? I am trying to explain as well as I can.

"The Mark, if you must know, is a black smudge at the base of the tail which tells the rest of the animal world that here is a creature of the deepest wisdom, and one blessed with the Sight. Now don't ask me what that is for I certainly don't know. All I do know is that I haven't got it.

"Anyway, Gabri it was who told me that I was to walk to the Moon. That, he told me, was my *Purpose*. Of course, I was shocked at first and couldn't understand what he was talking about and didn't really believe it anyhow. Gabri assured me that all sorts of creatures were doing it all the time. But, he added, the path was hard and difficult to follow.

"I asked Gabri if he knew how to get there, but he said that he had no idea, but was sure that it was my Purpose and that I should have no difficulty.

"When I pointed out that my bad leg would cause a problem, he just waved me aside saying that it was my Purpose to go and that it was somebody else's to help me.

"You see, Tomás, the problem with the truly wise is that they expect everyone to understand everything that they say immediately."

"And you haven't found anybody to help you?" Tomás asked.

"Well no," Don Alfonso agreed, after scratching himself, "because I have no idea who, or what, I am looking for."

"Didn't Gabri tell you?"

"No. As I told you about the truly wise, they are sometimes difficult to follow. Gabri just put it all down to Purpose and that was that. Everything would work out and here I am, still looking."

By this time it was late in the afternoon, Tomás looked up to where he had last seen his goats and, to his horror, they had disappeared. "The goats!" he cried. "They've all gone. I knew that I should have been watching them instead of listening to a foolish dog."

Don Alfonso howled at this insult. "You listened to me because you were supposed to," he told Tomás sharply. "I didn't force you, did I? Now, just you stay where you are and stop worrying about such a small matter, while I go and speak to your goats and bring them back. They look like a pretty reasonable bunch to me."

Tomás had little option but to trust the dog who he watched hobbling away up the slope, through the trees, until he too was gone. The boy sat down to imagine the good hiding he could expect if he returned to La Peña without the goats. Then, at just about the point when his thoughts had reached their darkest, he heard the unmistakable tinkle of goat bells and saw Don Alfonso and the billy goat chatting away further down the slope, followed by the rest of the flock who ambled along behind. Quickly Tomás counted them. They were all there, down to the smallest kid. Much relieved, he called down to Don Alfonso," "How did you do that? How did you find all the goats?"

Don Alfonso sighed. "Can you never accept what *is,* boy? This fine flock of goats is here because I asked them and, might I say, what an interesting flock of goats they are too," he added, carefully scanning the sky as he did so. "By the look of the day, Tomás, we had all better be on our way. For my part I really need something to eat and somewhere to rest." With that, Don Alfonso returned to his new friend the billy goat and their conversation, leaving Tomás to follow on as best he could.

That evening the boy made up a little bed of straw in his room for Don Alfonso to sleep on. Later on he brought back bread and some tasty sausage from the inn for them to share.

When at last his work was finally done and he could make his way wearily back to his room by the goat pen, Tomás was surprised to find Don Alfonso sitting on his bed gazing up at the moon. "Isn't she beautiful?" he said softly. "So still, so peaceful, so quiet, just hanging there in the blackness."

Tomás could not help but agree. The Moon had always strangely moved him, though he had never given it much thought until now.

"Would you like to go there?" Don Alfonso asked shortly.

"Me?"

"Why not?"

"Well," Tomás thought for a moment. There were thousands of perfectly good reasons why he could not go to the moon, or anywhere else for that matter, but he just couldn't think of any. "I don't know," he replied.

"Look, Tomás," Don Alfonso said, looking across at the boy through his sad, brown eyes. "What are you doing here? You work from dawn to late at night for your food and this miserable little room.

Every day is exactly the same. You are chained to a wall every bit as much as I was, and one day something dreadful will happen to you and you won't be able to move out of the way." Don Alfonso waved his limp paw to show what he meant. "Then, they will throw you out to fend for yourself. There are plenty of other orphans in Granada. Come with me, Tomás. Come with me to the Moon."

There was something in what Don Alfonso said that seemed true to Tomás. It was as if a little voice deep inside was speaking to him. He knew that Don Alfonso was right. Why shouldn't he walk to the Moon? Surely anywhere else would be better, even if they never actually made it as far as the Moon? Yet it was safe here, everyone knew him, he had food and shelter. Life could be better, true enough, but it could also be a whole lot worse. While his thoughts pulled him this way and that, the soft yellow moonlight streamed through the window and filled the room with peace. The Moon, so silent, so beautiful, hanging there in the blackness, wasn't that what Don Alfonso had said? Tomás would decide tomorrow. He was tired and was drifting off to sleep.

As Tomás closed his eyes, he seemed to hear a soft voice, a mother's voice calling out to him. "Tomás," the voice whispered softly, over and over again, "Tomás, you must come to me. You must come. You must come."

Suddenly he woke up and, rubbing the sleep from his eyes, saw the morning star shining brightly through his window while a cool breeze blowing in from the sierra filled the little room with the smell of pine trees.

Don Alfonso, meanwhile, lay sound asleep on his bed of straw. Tomás looked down at the sleeping dog and knew immediately what he had to do. "Don Alfonso," he called softly, "Don Alfonso."

The dog grunted as his sleep was broken, his eyes opened slowly. He said nothing.

"Don Alfonso," Tomás repeated, "Do you really think that it is possible to walk to the Moon?"

Don Alfonso raised his head thoughtfully. "Gabri told me so and I have no reason to doubt such a dog as he. Why?"

"Well, what I really mean is," Tomás began, "could we really walk to the Moon? When do you think we should start?"

Don Alfonso sat up and scratched himself vigorously for a few moments before replying. "Nothing like a good scratch first thing in the morning, especially when we have such a long journey ahead of us."

"What do you mean?" Tomás asked.

"What I mean, young Tomás, is that we should get started right away, before the sun gets too hot."

Tomás thought quickly. "I must get some food

together, and a blanket for the cold nights. Carmen is sure to have one. Then I will have to get a new pair of sandals, Francisco owes me a pair. Oh, of course, I shall have to tell everyone."

"Fine, fine," Don Alfonso replied airily. "While you're about your business, I'll just stop and have a quick word with the goats."

And so it was that Tomás and Don Alfonso began their great adventure: the boy and the dog who walked to the Moon!

Chapter Two

The Lady of the Snows

After the long and difficult climb that they had made since daybreak, Tomás and Don Alfonso sat together high up on the slopes of the great Sierra Nevada. From there they could look down on the city of Granada which bustled busily below them.

High in the clear blue sky a pair of eagles soared, their huge wings almost motionless as they rode the currents of warm air that rose from the plain far below.

As he looked down, Tomás could not help wondering what had brought him suddenly from the security of La Peña, making him homeless and friendless on the highest slopes of the Sierra Nevada. He watched as Don Alfonso rolled on his back, kicking his three good legs into the air. Tomás needed to blame someone for being where he was. "Do you know where we are going?" he asked irritably.

Don Alfonso finished his rolling and sat up. Looking directly at the boy he replied, with a twinkle in his eyes, "Yes and No." He paused. "Yes, in so far as we must find the Lady of the Snows, who lives up here somewhere, because wise old Gabri gave me a ring to give her by way of introduction. Look." Don Alfonso opened his mouth to let Tomás peer inside where, to his surprise, he saw a bright, delicately crafted gold ring fixed tightly round one of Don Alfonso's back teeth. "And no, I have no idea exactly where she is to be found."

Tomás shook his head in disbelief and asked, "Have you any idea just how big the Sierra Nevada is?"

"Have you?"

"No, but I have heard that it is very big, so it would take us forever to try and find this Lady of the Snows. That is, if she exists," the boy sneered.

"She exists alright," Don Alfonso told him firmly, "it was Gabri who told me about her and Gabri knows everything."

"But he didn't tell you where to find her."

"He didn't need to. We are meant to find the Lady of the Snows. After all, why would Gabri have given me this ring for her? So, just be patient and enjoy the view, something is bound to happen."

Something did. Suddenly, from the rocks just behind them, Tomás heard a great flapping of wings. He turned round in alarm to find the largest eagle that he had ever seen, perched within an arm's length of him, its sharp, yellow eyes fixed on him and the great, glistening beak glinting sharply in the sunshine.

The eagle ruffled his massive brown wings self-importantly. "I do not, as a rule, like humans," he announced in a very official way. "They are shifty and unreliable creatures. I would have been here earlier, dog," he said, turning to Don Alfonso, "but I was only told to pick up one dog; it says so here on this form." He fiddled beneath his feathers in an unsuccessful search for the paper. "Not to worry though, no one tells me anything. Can't get a straight answer from anybody. I am expected to be a mind-reader, I am."

"You know where to find the Lady of the Snows then?" Don Alfonso asked.

"Of course I do," the eagle snorted. "It was she herself who sent me to fetch you. She said nothing about any boy though."

"Tomás here is my assistant," Don Alfonso told him grandly. "As you can see, I have a little bit of a problem." He raised his bad leg for the eagle to see.

"Hmm," the eagle mused. "Do you have the ring?"

Don Alfonso opened his mouth so that the eagle could see the gold ring around his tooth.

After an especially careful inspection, the eagle seemed satisfied. Drawing himself up to his official height he said, "That all seems to be in order, but I still don't know what to do about the boy."

"What do you mean?" Don Alfonso asked.

"What I mean is simply this; I cannot carry you both up the mountain."

"Just tell us where to find the Lady of the Snows and we'll make our own way there," Don Alfonso suggested helpfully.

"Can't do that, squire, can't do that. Be more than my job's worth, Her Ladyship would have my feathers for dusters and no mistake. Just a minute." With that the eagle let out a piercing shriek that was, moments later, answered by a similar shriek from high above them. Almost immediately, they were joined by another eagle, equally large but less official.

The first eagle looked satisfied. "Very well," he said, "I shall carry the dog and my partner here will take the boy. Is that to your liking, dear?" he asked, turning to his partner.

"He is only a small, thin boy," the other replied, looking Tomás up and down with care. "It should be fairly easy provided he can hang on. You can hang on, can't you, boy?" she asked, turning to Tomás.

"I suppose so," he replied uncertainly.

"And how do you good eagles propose to carry me?" Don Alfonso asked.

"No problem, squire, carry you in these," the first eagle told him, brandishing one of his razor-sharp talons. Then, seeing how unhappy the idea made Don Alfonso, added, "You don't have to worry about these, my dear fellow. I can carry you high over these mountains without harming a hair on your precious head. Can't I, dear?" he asked, turning to his partner for support.

"Oh yes, dear, without harming a hair on his head." Don Alfonso remained unconvinced.

"Really, you won't notice a thing." the first eagle assured him.

"Not a thing," agreed the other.

"Just trust me, squire. The boy here is easy, all he has to do is to hang on to my partner's legs. Come along now," the eagle urged, "we haven't much time. Her Icy Imperial Highness, the Lady of the Snows commanded my speediest delivery and you have no idea how difficult she can be if her instructions are not obeyed to the letter. Besides, I have another delivery to make before I finish my shift."

"Is somebody else walking to the Moon?" Tomás asked.

"Creatures are always walking to the moon, squire," the eagle told him wearily. "All the time. You have no idea how boring it all is."

"Why do you do it then?"

"You have obviously never met Her Icy Imperial Highness, boy, otherwise you wouldn't ask. Now then, dog, be brave and come along, we must be on our way." Ignoring Don Alfonso's whimpered protests, the first eagle clasped him securely beneath the chest and, with a great fluster of wings, took off, soaring up towards the distant snowy peaks.

"Just take hold of my legs, boy," the remaining eagle commanded.

Tomás did as he was told and was very soon soaring up into the cold mountain air. He was amazed by all that he could see from this great height — there was the Plain of Granada stretching red and brown into the hazy distance; there were the tiny whitewashed villages; and, looking south, Tomás was amazed to make out the calm sea through the rising thermals. Above him the eagle's wings beat strongly as they travelled quickly over the snows.

After a short flight, they started to descend, lower and lower they dropped until Tomás found himself gently landing at the mouth of an ice cave that led down into the side of the mountain itself. To his great relief Don Alfonso had arrived safely too and was licking himself as if nothing in the world could be more normal than to be carried to the top of a mountain by a great eagle. Tomás waved goodbye as the eagle who had brought him took off once more, soon disappearing against the shadows of the sierras.

"Here we are then," Don Alfonso announced cheerfully. "Pleasant little flight that. Of course I had complete confidence in our fine feathered friends the Official Eagles."

Tomás laughed, "Of course you did, Don Alfonso. Of course you did. Though it didn't sound much like it when you took off," he added.

Don Alfonso finished licking and tugging at his coat. "Well," he said, standing up, "I suppose that we had better find the Lady of the Snows before it gets dark. We must trust in our Purpose." So with Purpose in mind he hobbled off into the cave.

The cave, in truth, was not really a cave at all, but more of a giant crack in a great wall of ice and quite large enough for Tomás and Don Alfonso to walk through. It was surprisingly light inside for a strange greenness shone through the smooth, cold walls of the cave. The further into the mountain they walked, the colder it became until, almost frozen, they staggered through the last of the light to find their way barred by a huge round boulder. They stopped, it was impossible to go any further, and decided there and then to retrace their steps back to the outer world. No sooner had they set off than the boulder which had barred their way rolled silently to one side to reveal another passageway that led deeper into the mountain. Without saying a word, Don Alfonso and Tomás walked through and, as silently as before, the boulder rolled back sealing them in. There was no turning back now.

The new passageway was even lighter than the

one that they had just left and they stopped for a few moments to take it all in. From the roof hung countless silver icicles that twinkled and shone in light that appeared to come from deep inside the shimmering ice walls.

"Come on," Don Alfonso whispered as he hobbled on ahead. Tomás followed, his imagination dancing amongst the changing patterns of light in that deep, green place.

The tunnel twisted into the rock for some distance before opening out to reveal the most incredible sight. In a cavern that was larger than any cathedral, and seemed to be the very belly of the mountain itself, they were amazed to see row upon row of fruit and nut trees stretched out before them. There were apples, oranges, peaches, apricots, cherries, bananas and almonds growing in profusion. From the ground grape vines twisted and climbed up into the trees bearing fat, red grapes in large, delicious bunches. There were so many types of bush and tree that Tomás was unable to put a name to most of them.

"Do you think it would be alright to try one of these apples?" Tomás asked softly, pointing to the nearest tree whose branches were covered with the most succulent fruit.

"I don't suppose that anybody would mind," Don Alfonso assured him absently.

Tomás was about to reach up and take one of the delicious red apples when, to his horror, a loud, icy voice rang out. "What do you think that you are doing there, boy?" it shrieked.

Tomás dropped his hand and looked about him for the source of the voice.

"What do you mean by coming here and helping yourself to my fruit?" it continued.

"I wasn't ... I didn't ..." Tomás tried to explain.

"Don't give me your excuses," thundered the voice. "Come over here immediately."

"But where are you?" Tomás called out fearfully.

"Over here you stupid boy. Here! And look lively about it too."

The boy looked round only to find Don Alfonso hiding behind his legs. "What are you doing?" he hissed. "You got us here. What are we going to do?"

"Run away," Don Alfonso offered unhelpfully.

"And where are we going to run to?"

Before Don Alfonso could reply, the voice boomed out once more: "I am waiting. I am not accustomed to being kept waiting. Now come over here. IMMEDIATELY!!"

Fearfully Don Alfonso and Tomás made their way through the vast orchard. All around them trees grew, some in fruit, some in flower. The fragrance they gave off, even in this vast cavern, was almost overpowering. However, the fearful pair were much too worried about what was going to happen to think about things like that.

Though it seemed much longer, it was only a

few minutes later that, a little way over to his right, Tomás saw what appeared to be a crystal staircase that rose sparkling through the trees. Drawn towards it in wonder, they could only stand and gaze upwards in astonishment at the shining, spiralling crystal staircase, that soared like a curved blade of ice high above the trees, reaching up towards the invisible roof of the cavern. From the ground it was just possible to make out the distant figure of a woman dressed in a long white robe, sitting regally on a throne of ice that shimmered in uncountable colours.

The Lady of the Snows stood up and called down to where Tomás and Don Alfonso were standing at the foot of the staircase, "Well, what have you got to say for yourselves?"

"We fling ourselves down at your mercy, O Eighth Wonder of the World," Don Alfonso replied, before rolling on his back and kicking his three good legs into the air.

"Oh get up, and stop grovelling," the Lady of the Snows replied irritably. "Where have you been all this time, Don Alfonso?"

"She knows who you are!" Tomás exclaimed in surprise.

"Of course I know who he is," the Lady of the Snows snorted. "Now get on with it, Don Alfonso."

The dog scrambled to his feet as well as he could. "Well Your Imperial Whiteness," he whined, "I was delayed by this poor leg, as you can see."

"Tish! Tush!" boomed Her Imperial Whiteness. "You were sent this wretched boy to help you."

"Yes, indeed, Your Highness and Whiteness," Don Alfonso grovelled. "Of course, you are right." Without looking away from the distant white figure, he whispered through his teeth to Tomás, "Get down on your knees quickly, this is going to take some talking. She's worse than I expected."

Don Alfonso waited briefly until Tomás was kneeling beside him before continuing. "Your Graciousness must understand that we poor creatures before you imperfectly understood what Gabri the Wise told us."

"What will she do?" Tomás whispered.

"Kill us probably."

Further speculation was useless, the voice boomed out once more, "I would have thought it would have been plain to an idiot. Come up here and let me take a look at you."

Don Alfonso looked towards the shining staircase of crystal and then up at Tomás. "I fear that my poor leg prevents me from climbing up to your delightful presence, Your Wonderfulness."

"The boy will have to carry you then. Now come up here and be quick about it," was the short reply.

Without saying another word, Tomás picked up his scrawny, brown friend and set off up the staircase.

"Don't look down," Don Alfonso warned him before tightly shutting his own eyes.

It took them some time to climb up to the throne, but from the wide platform on which it stood, Tomás could look out on the forest beneath and understood better the soft, green light that shone from the walls of the cavern.

The Lady of the Snows was very small in comparison to the huge throne of coloured ice on which she sat; no taller, in fact, than Tomás. She wore a long, white dress of a heavy, silken material trimmed with white fur, almost the same shade as her hair. What was striking about the Lady of the Snows, were her fine, long fingers covered by a remarkable collection of rings that shone golden, heavy with precious stones of every shape and colour.

"Well?" she asked, wagging a jewelled finger at them.

Don Alfonso paused for a few moments before replying, "Yes." he announced firmly. "Yes indeed. I now know that Gabri the Wise spoke only the truth when he described your wisdom and beauty."

The Lady of the Snows smiled for the first time. "Dear Gabri," she mused. "Such a well-bred dog."

Don Alfonso sensed his opportunity; "Oh most certainly, Your Icyness. Gabri assured me on more than one occasion of the wonderful grace, beauty and mercy of the Lady of the Snows."

The Lady of the Snows beamed down, her smile revealing teeth jagged as a saw, that shone white and sharp. "Now give me my ring," she demanded.

Innocently Don Alfonso presented his open mouth so that the Lady of the Snows might easily take the ring, and was stunned when she screamed at him, "Who do you think I am, some sort of servant? I am not accustomed to fiddling around in dogs' mouths. Boy," she turned to Tomás, "take the ring from that dog's mouth and present it to me properly."

Fearfully, Tomás did as he was told and, rubbing the ring on his sleeve to polish it up a bit, finally presented the delicate little ring to its new owner. The Lady of the Snows slipped the ring on to her little finger and held it away from her as she admired the colour and texture of it. "So," she said at length, "you wish my permission to walk to the Moon, I take it?"

"Oh yes, please," Tomás replied enthusiastically, adding more cautiously, "Do many people walk to the Moon?"

The Lady of the Snows laughed. "Goodness me, child, all manner of creatures walk to the Moon, though sadly all too few of your species. Human people, you see, have forgotten the Great Law of the Learned Pibroch Rat and do not believe. You believe though, don't you, boy?" she added.

"Oh yes, Your Majesty, we both do," Tomás

replied, though he had no idea what she was talking about.

The Lady of the Snows relaxed, smiled once more and clapped her hands. "Good, good. Now I want you to listen carefully to what I am going to tell you for I am not in the habit of repeating myself. Do I make myself clear?"

Tomás nodded vigorously while Don Alfonso said nothing.

The Lady of the Snows continued with her instructions: "When you return to the orchard below you will find a large sack. You will take this sack to the Tree of Desire and fill it with all those things that you think necessary for the next stage of your journey. Once you have done this then you may help yourself to as much fruit as you wish. Boys, I know, like fruit.

"When you have eaten your fill and rested, you will make your way to the Enchanted Passage of the Snow Grapes where you will find a small, green door. Behind this door is a passage that will lead you out on to the Sierra once more. From there you must seek out the Wild Weaver of the Alpujarras, who holds the key to the Great Sub-terranean Lake which you must cross to reach the Springtime."

"Your Sublime Whiteness is too kind," Don Alfonso fawned.

"How do we find the Wild Weaver of the Alpujarras, your Majesty?" Tomás asked tentatively.

"You must watch the sky carefully for a storm that builds far out to sea and sweeps in bringing the life-giving rain with it. When this storm reaches you, you must find its edge and follow it to where the rainbow begins, and there you will surely find the Weaver."

Tomás was just about to ask another question when, abruptly, the Lady of the Snows stood up and, waving her jewel-encrusted hands, screamed at them: "GO! and be quick about it. I want no more of your questions. I wish to be alone with the ring that dear, dear Gabri has sent me."

In sudden clap of thunder she was gone, and Tomás and Don Alfonso found themselves standing once more amongst the most fragrant fruit trees that anyone could imagine. Almost immediately Tomás started to eat the fruit which hung down from the trees: apples, pears, oranges, bananas. So preoccupied was he that he quite forgot Don Alfonso who needed his most mournful howl to draw the boy's attention. "Steady on, Tomás," he cautioned. "We have to find the Tree of Desire first."

The boy stopped, and trying to swallow a mouthful of banana, spluttered, "The what?"

"The Tree of Desire, or had you forgotten?"

Suddenly Tomás remembered, shaking his head with embarrassment. "Oh yes," he mumbled.

"You must be careful, Tomás," Don Alfonso warned him. "You must only do exactly what the

Lady of the Snows tells you and not be tempted, otherwise you will lose your memory forever. The Lady of the Snows said that you could eat your fill only once we had found the Tree of Desire." Without saying another word, Don Alfonso hobbled off down a pathway that ran between two ancient walnut trees. Tomás had no choice but to follow, quite forgetting the large brown sack that lay on the ground nearby.

They were eventually drawn by the sound of running water, to a grove, deep within the orchard. There, on the banks of a beautifully clear stream that gushed out of the cavern floor, stood a stunted, wizened tree that was twisted and blackened, and looked most sad and forgotten. "That," Don Alfonso announced, "is the Tree of Desire."

Tomás was amazed. "The Tree of Desire!" he gasped. "I expected something a bit different, golden perhaps, with leaves of silver at the very least. Not this rotten old thing."

No sooner had the words left his mouth than, to his utter astonishment, the tree suddenly changed, standing there shimmering gold with leaves of the purest silver, that sparkled and shone on every branch.

"The Tree of Desire, as I told you," Don Alfonso told him smugly, "as Her Worshipfulness told us. This tree, as you can see, responds immediately to your slightest desire. By the way, did you bring the sack?"

Tomás shook his head. He remembered seeing a large brown sack when they returned to the orchard, but had forgotten all about it. "No," he admitted. "I was too busy eating."

Don Alfonso howled his disappointment. "You must listen to what you are told, Tomás. What are we going to do now?"

Tomás sighed and shrugged his shoulders. "I suppose that I shall have to go back and find it," he replied.

Don Alfonso chuckled. "No need," he told him. "Just think about it. Think hard."

Tomás thought about the large, brown sack that he could clearly see in his mind's eye, lying at the foot of the crystal staircase. Barely had the sack taken shape in his mind than it suddenly appeared on the ground before him. Not really believing it to be true, Tomás bent down and quickly picked up the sack, running his hand over the coarse material to make sure that it was real.

"Tree of Desire," Don Alfonso reminded him.

"You mean that I only have to think of something, anything, and it will appear?"

"That's what Trees of Desire generally do," Don Alfonso replied.

Tomás was still not convinced, and said so. Don Alfonso shook his head wearily, wondering what further proof his young friend needed. "The problem with you humans is that you just cannot accept what *is*. Listen, Tomás, just try this for size: think of what you most like to eat; doesn't matter what it is, just think about it," he said.

"I like sardines," Tomás mused, "nice big ones, fried in olive oil."

"Well just think about them," Don Alfonso told him.

Tomás closed his eyes tightly and thought; in his mind he could see a large blue plate which was entirely covered in the most perfectly fried sardines. So vividly did the boy imagine the cooked fish that he even thought he could smell them. He opened his eyes in astonishment, for there on the ground before him, was the same plate covered with the same sardines, exactly as he had imagined them.

"There you are," Don Alfonso beamed. "Now eat them. It's my turn now. Let me see, I think that I would like a nice juicy leg bone full of marrow."

He had barely finished speaking when there appeared before him the largest, tastiest looking bone that Tomás had ever seen. Don Alfonso settled himself down in front of his prize, resting his good leg on it to keep it steady and drawing his long, pink tongue along its length. Then, aware that Tomás was staring at him with disbelief, snapped, "What are you gawping at, boy? Eat your fish. Bone-eating deserves my full concentration."

Tomás turned his attention to his sardines while Don Alfonso lay down gnawing contentedly at his bone.

Some time later, when both had finished eating, Don Alfonso and Tomás had to decide what they needed to continue their journey.

"Some warm clothes and new shoes for me, of course. A compass, a big one like the one that I saw in a shop in Granada," Tomás began.

Don Alfonso shook his head, "Wait a minute, wait a minute," he interrupted to cut Tomás short. "Who is going to carry all of this?"

This thought made Tomás realize just how impractical most of the things that he wanted were. "What do you think we need, Don Alfonso?" he asked.

"Well," he began, "what we really need is some food; a good loaf and some tasty sausage will do — and, oh yes, you must have a good strong knife, you never know when one of those might come in useful. Can't think of anything else, can you?"

Tomás was amazed. "Is that all you want?" he asked. "This tree can grant us anything we want, and all that you can suggest is a loaf and some sausage?"

"Tasty sausage," Don Alfonso corrected him. "Tomás, are you really going to weigh yourself down with your desires?"

"How do you mean?"

"Sit down a moment and I shall tell you," Don Alfonso instructed him. "Tomás, have you ever wanted anything really badly, so badly that you couldn't get it out of your mind?"

44

Tomás thought about it for a moment or two before replying, "I suppose so," he agreed and told Don Alfonso how he had once seen a thick leather belt with a silver buckle in a shop that he often passed on his errands for Carmen, and had decided that he had to have it.

"And did you get it?"

"Yes, but I had to work very hard you know, to get the money to buy it."

"Where is this belt now?"

Tomás laughed out loud. It dawned on him just what Don Alfonso was talking about. "It broke," he admitted ruefully, "it broke, and I had to throw it out."

"And then you went on to desire something else? You see, Tomás, desire is like a dead weight that slows you down. You want something. You get it and you become bored with it, or it breaks and is thrown away. The Tree of Desire is a test. You must tread lightly on the Earth taking only what you need, not what you want.

"On this journey we will often be tested like this but, if we learn the lessons, we will succeed in what we are doing. But we must always keep our wits about us."

Tomás knew that what Don Alfonso had told him was the truth. "A loaf?" he repeated.

"Yes."

"Some sausage?"

"Tasty sausage. The kind that has no gristle in it and just melts in the mouth."

"And a good strong knife with a sharp blade?"

"Exactly."

Tomás thought hard and, sure enough, on the ground in front of them lay the bread, the sausage and the most magnificent knife that Tomás had ever seen, in a strong leather sheath too. Hurriedly he stuffed the bread and the sausage into the sack and strapped the knife to his waist.

"Good," Don Alfonso said admiringly. "Now, we must be on our way. By the way, you can eat as much fruit as you want to now. You still like fruit, don't you?"

Tomás certainly did and started to eat, not as he had done the first time, but carefully, taking only what he needed and putting a few choice fruits into the sack for later on.

After walking through the orchard for some time, the pair came to a strange, tangled thicket of vines. These were not the vines that Tomás was accustomed to seeing; the leaves were bright blue and the large succulent bunches of grapes were as clear as raindrops. These were Snow Grapes. As he reached out to take one, Don Alfonso shook his head. "Only the Lady of the Snows can eat those without losing her memory. The snow grapes are the final test here, thank goodness."

"How do you know all this?" Tomás asked as they scrambled through the vines.

"Gabri told me," Don Alfonso puffed. "He warned me about the Lady of the Snows. Full of tricks, he said."

They followed the little path, tangled and overgrown as it twisted through the snow vines until they came at last to a small green door in the ice wall. Carefully Tomás turned the handle and pulled. Slowly the door opened and before them lay a long passage brightly lit by torches of burning tallow.

Don Alfonso led the way. Tomás was just about to follow when a familiar voice boomed out from nowhere, "And close the door behind you!"

Tomás obeyed this last order of the Lady of the Snows gratefully. He was relieved to at last be free of her strange, icy realm, but a little fearful of what they might find at the end of this tunnel.

The tunnel, though brightly lit, was long and twisting. They had walked along it for some time when Tomás thought that he heard something breathing behind them. "Don Alfonso, I think we're being followed!" he hissed. "Listen!"

They both strained their ears, but could hear nothing but themselves. Finally Don Alfonso shook his head. "It's just your imagination, Tomás," he said. "I think that we must both be hearing things. Come on, let's get out of here."

It only took them a short while until they were climbing out of the tunnel into the sunlight of a late autumn afternoon. They were both too relieved to be in the outside world once more to notice that the tunnel that they had recently scrambled from had disappeared back into the mountainside.

Without saying a word, the two friends moved off to seek shelter amongst the nearby rocks where they could share some bread and sausage, and decide what to do next.

Far below them, small white farmhouses sat amongst a web of fields, orchards and irrigation channels. Tomás could easily imagine the activities that were going on down there as the hard work of the day drew to a close. He felt just a little homesick and lost for a moment.

Don Alfonso seemed to understand, telling him softly, "We're both wanderers you know, Tomás; you and me. That's our Purpose, you see. Besides, I know that I wouldn't be happy chained up in some yard waiting for any scraps that someone thought to give me."

As he listened to Don Alfonso's gentle voice, so the sadness lifted, giving way slowly to hope and expectation. Tomás gave his friend a big hug and had his face well licked in return. As the sun was setting far out to sea, the boy and the dog settled themselves down amongst the rocks to sleep. It had been a long day.

Chapter Three

The Wild Weaver
of the Alpujarras

The sun rose from behind the high peaks that towered above them. Tomás awoke first and took out some bread from his sack before gently shaking Don Alfonso, who was curled up beside him.

Don Alfonso opened an eye, raised his head and yawned. "Day already," he observed, taking the bread that was being offered to him.

"What are we to do now?" Tomás asked as he ate.

"Wait for a storm to blow in from the sea I suppose," Don Alfonso replied.

"Anyway, who is this Wild Weaver of the Alpujarras that we're supposed to find?"

Don Alfonso sat up and looked up at the clear, cloudless sky and out to the distant sea. "Gabri told me that he weaves the rainbows," he said.

"He does what?" Tomás asked in disbelief. Though the Lady of the Snows had mentioned this fact, Tomás — in the manner of boys — had not been listening.

"Rainbows," Don Alfonso replied calmly. "He weaves them. Have you never seen a rainbow?"

"Of course I have."

"And have you never thought about who weaves them?"

"They're not woven!" Tomás snorted.

"Well how are they made then?"

Tomás thought for a moment and had to admit that he knew nothing at all about rainbows.

"There you are!" Don Alfonso replied with some satisfaction. "Jumping to conclusions again. The trouble with humans, in my experience, is that they think that they have all the answers when, in truth, they don't even know the questions."

"And dogs do?"

"Gabri certainly does. I would never make such a claim for myself, as you know."

Tomás was becoming a little annoyed with his friend, and asked sharply, "Why do we have to see this Weaver anyway?"

"Have you ever seen a road without signposts?"

"No."

"Well then, look on the Weaver as a signpost."

Tomás smiled. Don Alfonso seemed to have an answer for everything. "You sound as if you know him," he said.

"I only know what Gabri told me. I thought it a bit odd myself at the time."

"Will you tell me about Gabri?" Tomás asked, as they watched the sun rise over the sea.

"Gabri," Don Alfonso mused. "Why he's just a sheepdog, a big, white sheepdog with a black patch at the base of his tail. He knows everything about everything, and that is the truth."

Suddenly, tugging at his friend's sleeve, he pointed with his nose towards the sea. "Hey, Tomás," he exclaimed "Look out there!"

"Where?"

"Out there, on the horizon."

Tomás strained his eyes and, sure enough far out to sea he could just make out a smudge of black cloud that had formed, and was now rolling into the coast on a cool sea breeze.

From where they sat, high in the sierra, Tomás and Don Alfonso had plenty of time to watch the coming storm as it developed, while they ate up what remained of the food brought from the Lady of the Snows' cavern.

The storm strengthened alarmingly, steadily becoming wilder and blacker as it approached, pushing before it a strong, cold wind that moaned among the rocks where they sat. Once it crossed the coast, Tomás could easily see the rain pouring steadily from the clouds. There followed a crackle of lightning that flashed from the deepest blackness and a long roll of thunder that echoed through the hills. Closer and closer the storm approached until the rain lashed the lower slopes of the sierra.

Don Alfonso sniffed at the air and cocked his head as he carefully watched the passage of the storm. Then, turning quickly to Tomás, he urged speed, adding: "We must find the edge of the storm!"

"Why?" Tomás asked breathlessly, as he followed Don Alfonso who hobbled with remarkable speed between the rocks.

"We have to find the edge. Now quickly, follow me!"

Very soon they were being soaked by the rainstorm as it passed up the slope. Almost as suddenly as it had engulfed them, so the storm passed leaving them in the dry. Tomás could see the edge now but had little time to wonder at it for Don Alfonso was scampering up the slope at the same pace as the storm, but just managing to keep on the dry side. Tomás followed, but was quite mystified by what was going on.

Leading the way, carefully keeping to the very edge of the storm, Don Alfonso ran onwards and upwards over the high, sharp rocks until, near the summit of the sierra, they were astonished to see the most magnificent rainbow that rose and soared into the stormy sky from behind a huge boulder high on the ridge.

"That's it!" Don Alfonso shouted excitedly. "That's where the Weaver lives! We've found him!"

Breathless from running up the steep slope, they at last reached the boulder, by which time

the storm had passed and was now driving onwards taking much-needed rain to the farmers
inland. From where Tomás and Don Alfonso stood
to catch their breath, their gaze was drawn to a
tiny, multicoloured hut that stood on what appeared to be four gigantic chicken legs. Beneath
the hut, stacked in a jumble, were many bales of
woollen yarn in — not surprisingly — all the
colours of the rainbow.

From inside the hut there came the most fearful
clattering and banging while, out of a large hole
in the roof, there emerged the clearest, finest
rainbow imaginable that stretched upwards in a
great shining arc until it disappeared into the
distance. As they watched, a spindly figure in
green breeches and a long tailed coat of the same
colour dashed out of the hut and slid down a rope
to the ground, where he immediately began
rummaging round in the wool store tossing coloured bales about him in his hunt. After a few
moments, he emerged with a ball of blue wool
which he attached to a hook at the end of the rope
and, satisfied that the yarn was secure, he scrambled back up the rope to his hut drawing the yarn
up after him before disappearing with it back into
the hut where the clattering and banging began
once more.

At last the noise stopped and the rainbow began
to melt away into the clear, fresh light of the day.
Tomás and Don Alfonso watched as the spindly

figure emerged from the hut once more, paused to look out towards the sea, shook his head and called out, "You've arrived, I see."

Tomás looked down at Don Alfonso, waiting for him to react but, before he could do so the strange figure stamped his foot, causing the whole rickety structure on which he stood to shake: "Come over here, the pair of you, and be quick about it. There's another storm on the way. Quickly!" he shouted.

Neither Tomás nor Don Alfonso needed further bidding and ran to the hut as quickly as they could.

"Are you the Wild Weaver of the Alpujarras?" Don Alfonso called up.

The figure tossed down the rope once more before replying, "Of course I'm the Wild Weaver of the Alpujarras. Who were you expecting to find?"

There was no reply to this, instead they both looked up and saw the Weaver gazing far out to sea before returning his attention to them. "Quickly now!" he called down. "Shin up this rope. There's another storm due soon."

"I fear that will be impossible, sir," Don Alfonso called out sadly. "You see I have an injured leg."

"Well, the boy should tie the rope around your waist and I shall pull you up. Now be quick about it for we haven't much time."

Tomás did as he was told, and very soon Don Alfonso was swinging up towards the platform.

Once Don Alfonso had safely arrived, the Weaver swung down the rope once more. "While you're there, young man, bring up a ball of green with you, please."

Tomás looked at the bales of yarn that were strewn about beneath the hut and pulled out a ball of green which he held triumphantly over his head.

"Good," the Weaver acknowledged. "Now climb up here. Your friend and I will be inside."

With some difficulty, Tomás scrambled up the rope to the top. From the platform he looked out across the peaks and, sure enough, there was another black cloud rapidly approaching from the south-west bringing thunder and lightning with it. Without further pause, he dashed in through the door to find the Wild Weaver of the Alpujarras sitting at his rickety weaving frame ready to begin. He handed him the ball of green wool and watched in amazement as the Weaver's feet began frantically to work the treadles.

Tomás barely had time to take in his surroundings when the Weaver called for more yarn; red and indigo this time. Without question, Tomás hurried from the hut, sliding down the rope to the ground. There was no time to examine the contents of the wool store because the storm was almost upon them, and from above came the sound of furious clattering as the Weaver treadled his loom. Nearby, amongst a confusion of colours and half-opened bales of yarn, Tomás saw the balls of red and took one down. Indigo was a bit more difficult; he had no idea what indigo looked like, and had never thought to ask. He was just about to despair when he heard a voice, a gentle, calm voice, calling out to him. "Next to the blue," it said.

Tomás saw the blue wool and also saw a similar colour, but just a little more purple, in the bale next to it. "Is that indigo?" he called out.

"Yes," replied the voice.

Tomás took down the ball of indigo wool. "Thanks," he shouted, before scurrying back to the rope where he attached the balls of wool to the hook. Then, as the Weaver had done before, Tomás clambered up the rope to the platform, drawing the wool behind him. He was just in time too, for by now the rain was hammering down on the roof. The Weaver offered no thanks, but simply took the balls of wool and added them to those he was working with.

Tomás had barely caught his breath when the Weaver called out once more, "Quickly, boy, some yellow and some orange while you're about it."

Once more, Tomás slid down the rope and, after some tugging and pulling at bales, finally located the yellow and the orange. As quickly as he could, and despite the pouring rain, Tomás scrambled back up the rope with the wool. He pushed open the door and paused for a moment to watch the strangest sight he had ever seen. For there, at the rather ramshackle loom, sat the Weaver wildly working his treadle, his long arms and legs waving up and down as the shuttle sped first one way, and then the other. He watched spellbound as the new rainbow soared upwards through the roof in delicately woven bands of colour; red, orange, yellow, green, blue, indigo and violet. Tomás had never seen anything like it. He had seen many rainbows before, when he had been out on the sierras with Fat Francisco's goats, but had never thought where they came from until now. He would never have imagined that they were woven!

As he watched, so Tomás noticed that the rain seemed to be lifting until the loud drumming on the roof stopped and the Weaver rested at his loom. "Perfect, perfect!" he exclaimed, happily clapping his hands. "Good job you were here to help, young man. Did you find the colours that I asked for easily enough?"

"Oh yes," Tomás assured him. Then he remembered the voice. "I wouldn't have found the indigo though if you hadn't told me where it was."

The Weaver turned on his stool and looked at the boy, as Don Alfonso stirred from the blanket on which he was dozing in a corner of the hut, "I didn't tell you where indigo was, boy," the Weaver remarked. "Why, I was much to busy to notice."

"Was it you, Don Alfonso?" Tomás asked.

Don Alfonso yawned. "Not me, Tomás," he said. "It must have been your imagination."

"I'm sure that I didn't imagine it," Tomás said, though he admitted to himself that so many strange things had happened to him recently that maybe he had. So, he decided to put it to the back of his mind.

The Weaver leapt nimbly from his stool and ran for the door where he looked out over the sierra and beyond to the sea. "No more today," he told them. "Besides it will soon be evening and you never see rainbows at night, do you?"

Tomás admitted that he had never seen a rainbow at night. The Weaver clapped his hands in delight. "What a bright boy you are. Just a pity we don't get more people through here. Now we must eat, and you and Don Alfonso must rest for tomorrow you face the next part of your journey."

"What is the next part?" Tomás asked.

The Weaver sat down once more on his stool and crossed his thin legs before replying, "Oh, only the Great Subterranean Lake."

"The Great Subterranean Lake?" Tomás repeated.

"Yes."

"Where is it?" he asked.

"Beneath the ground. Right down there." The Weaver jabbed a long, bony finger downwards to make his point.

"You mean to say that there is a lake down there, beneath our feet, and we have to cross it?"

"Certainly. I don't know of any other way to get to the Moon, unless you do."

Don Alfonso howled his hungry howl. "Tomás, Tomás, why do you ask so many questions? Can't you concentrate on something important, like food, say?"

"Did you know all this Don Alfonso?" Tomás asked, ignoring his friend's request.

"Only the little that Gabri told me. I didn't think to question it because he had said that such a place exists, and who am I to question a dog with the Mark on him?"

Tomás realized that he would learn little more from either Don Alfonso or the Weaver, but something troubled him, and he had to ask one last question: "How do we get there?"

"Down the Well!" the Weaver answered brightly, as he leapt from his stool and rummaged amongst his cooking utensils for a big iron cooking pot.

That night, after a hearty meal of chickpeas and rice, Tomás, Don Alfonso, and the Weaver sat around the cosy fire that blazed in one corner of the hut talking over their experiences of the day, while outside the soft, peaceful Moon shone down on the ragged peaks.

"Why do you weave rainbows?" Tomás asked.

The Weaver thought for a moment and smiled, "Who else would weave them?" he replied.

From the blanket on which he was comfortably curled, Don Alfonso explained, "I am very much afraid, my dear Weaver, that there are things that humans, in general, stoutly refuse to accept or understand. Now," he turned to Tomás, "could you possibly imagine a storm without there being a rainbow at the end of it? I mean to say, how would we know if it was over?"

"I'd never thought about it," his friend admitted.

"Well, you must thank the Weaver."

"I suppose so," Tomás agreed sheepishly.

"Tomás," the Weaver said. "You know that we are all here for a reason, we all have a Purpose. Mine, you see, is to weave rainbows; yours is to help Don Alfonso to walk to the Moon; Don Alfonso's is to help you. We are all part of the same whole, like the colours of the rainbow — we exist separately, but together. Can you understand that?"

"Yes, but I can't see why walking to the Moon should be important to anyone."

The Weaver added another log to the fire which spat and crackled, sending sparks dancing in the darkness up the chimney. "No one knows what is or isn't important. All purposes are of equal importance, otherwise they wouldn't be there."

This was all too much for Tomás; it was making his head spin. "How much further do we have to go?" he asked.

The Weaver laughed, "You have a long way to

travel yet. The difficult parts of the journey are only just beginning, for you must now cross the Great Subterranean Lake that I told you of, in order to reach Springtime in the high Guadar-ramas."

"And after that?"

The Weaver shook his head. "That I cannot tell you, for it is my task simply to point the way, not to describe the road."

"Tomorrow, will you show us the well?" Tomás asked sleepily, noticing that Don Alfonso was curled up and fast asleep on his blanket.

"Tomorrow," the Weaver agreed. "Now you must rest. You have a long way to go."

Chapter Four

Journey to the Great Subterranean Lake

The next morning, bright and early, just as the sun rose above the peaks, Tomás, Don Alfonso and the Weaver shared a breakfast of goat's cheese and bread followed by large, steaming mugs of sweet manzanilla tea, before leaving the hut for the well that would lead them to the Great Subterranean Lake.

In the fresh morning light, the three followed a well-worn path that twisted along a rocky ridge to where there stood a tripod of three stout poles, lashed together over a deep, dark hole from which a large wooden bucket swung down from the centre on a length of stout rope.

"Right!" the Weaver asked cheerfully as they drew closer. "Who's first? Come along now. Hop into the bucket, one of you."

"After you, Tomás, my dear boy." Don Alfonso

urged while retreating a little from the edge of the well.

"Me?"

"It's my leg, Tomás, you understand," he whined.

"I don't see what that has to do with it," Tomás replied sharply. However, seeing that he had no other choice, he clambered uneasily into the bucket.

Almost at once the Weaver took up the rope and started to lower the boy down into the well. Tomás felt a great fear in his stomach as he was lowered deeper and deeper into the dripping darkness. There was no sign of anything below him, only the silent blackness. Shortly though a change began to occur; the air which had earlier been damp and cold became gradually drier and warmer. For an instant, Tomás thought that he could even smell lavender and roses. Lower and lower the bucket lurched until he could see a faint light far below him. The further he went, so the light became brighter, the air warmer and the scent of flowers stronger until finally, with a jolt that all but tipped him from the bucket, Tomás arrived at the bottom. He could only gaze out in wonder at the view before him.

He had landed on a grassy hill that overlooked a limitless lake of turquoise water, that stretched like a sheet of polished glass to a distant horizon.

Above him beige clouds hung motionless in a yellow sky.

Fearfully Tomás stepped from the bucket. The ground beneath his feet was firm and the air smelled sweet. So amazed was he by what he saw that he hardly noticed the bucket as it swung upwards on its return journey.

Some time afterwards, Don Alfonso arrived whimpering pitifully in the bottom of the bucket where he lay huddled, his eyes tightly closed. With a loud crash, the bucket landed tipping its unfortunate occupant out on to the grass. Once Don Alfonso realized that he had arrived safely and, as always, being aware of his dignity, he scrambled to his feet with a little help from Tomás. "We are here, I see," he announced, shaking himself vigorously.

"And there goes the bucket," Tomás replied as the bucket swung its way back to the surface.

Even Don Alfonso appeared overawed by the appearance of the lake, and by the puffs of beige cloud that floated in the yellow sky. They had arrived at the Great Subterranean Lake, but what next?

Chapter Five

The Law of the Learned
Pibroch Rat

Tomás and Don Alfonso sat for some time without
speaking. Once the bucket had clattered back up
the shaft to the surface they were left in a silence
so complete that they both felt that they could
hear themselves thinking! There was no wind to
wave the grass, to set the flowers nodding or even
to disturb the mirrored surface of the turquoise
lake.

They had been watching the scene for some
time when both became aware of a rustling and a
rushing sound just out of sight, beyond a little
headland that jutted out into the smooth water.
As they listened so the noise grew steadily louder
until, much to their surprise, an odd little boat
sailed round the headland and made its way, none
too smoothly, towards the beach just below where
Tomás and Don Alfonso were sitting.

A strange craft it was too: bright green, it was

driven by two large, red paddle wheels that churned the turquoise water into a white foam that left a zigzag course in its wake. The reason for this soon became clear the closer the boat came to the shore, because the paddle wheels were being turned by a pair of large brown rats running in wheels in-board of the paddles, while another rat clung to an over-large tiller bar that controlled the rudder.

Unable to resist a closer look at this strange craft and its crew, Tomás and Don Alfonso hurried down to the shore where they were able to watch the ragged seamanship of the three rats more closely.

"Oh do try and keep up, Moravia dear," the helmsrat called out.

"It isn't Moravia's fault, Agamemnon old chap, but mine I fear," the rat powering one of the wheels called out.

"How silly of me, Hector," the rat in the other wheel admitted. "I don't know why I can't keep my mind on what I am doing."

"Don't trouble yourself, Moravia," the helmsrat assured her. "I think we are all having a wretched time of it. Come along, Hector luvvy! Please try and concentrate!"

The boat only zigzagged all the more as the two rats in the wheels tried, but failed, to run at the same speed, while the helmsrat tried to correct their course, by swinging furiously on the tiller bar. Gradually they neared the shore when the helmsrat suddenly realized that they were about to crash into the beach, and started running up and down the deck squeaking loudly: "Now then, you two, if you would be so kind as to reverse. I fear that we are going to crash."

"Now, you mean Agamemnon?" one of the others called from a wheel.

"If you don't mind awfully, Moravia dear," the helmsrat replied.

"The shore seems very close to me, Agamemnon," the rat in the other wheel observed lazily.

"You're right, Hector, it does seem a trifle close," Agamemnon agreed.

"What shall we do?" asked the first rat.

"I think it might be useful if we reverse," Agamemnon suggested.

"Come along, Hector, if you agree, then we should really try running backwards," the rat called Moravia offered.

"Why?"

There was no time for an answer as the little green craft ploughed into the shore, throwing Agamemnon into the water, and the other two into a heap on the deck.

Tomás and Don Alfonso ran down the beach to offer their help and were just in time to lift Agamemnon from the water, and return him, soaking wet, to the deck.

Agamemnon shook himself dry and looked at

the new arrivals. "Many thanks to you two," he said. "I am afraid that I am in a rather dishevelled state and cannot properly greet you."

"No, quite right," the other rats agreed, untangling themselves from the heap where they had landed.

"We don't mind," Tomás said helpfully.

Agamemnon looked at his fellow crew members. "I suppose that if I apologized, then I might greet the visitors?"

"What do you think, Moravia?" Hector asked.

"Oh you know that I always defer to you in matters of etiquette, Hector."

"If you would excuse us for a moment, gentlemen," Agamemnon said, "we shall go below and take a vote on it."

With that the three rats scurried down a hatch and disappeared inside the boat, leaving Tomás and Don Alfonso standing in the water.

They were about to scramble back on to the shore when the rats re-emerged on to the deck led by Agamemnon, who was obviously the spokesrat. "Ahem," he began officially. "Following a unanimous vote on the subject, it has been decided that you can be greeted officially. So, Greetings!" The other two clapped politely, nodding their heads in agreement.

"Now then," Moravia said. "Are you two gentlemen walking to the Moon?"

"Indeed we are, madam," Don Alfonso replied.

"In that case you had better come aboard, and we can get under way," she told them.

Tomás shook his head. "How are you going to get the boat away? It seems to me to be stuck fast."

The rats looked bewildered for a moment, then, as a group, they dashed to the bows and looked down into the water where, to their horror, they found that what Tomás had said was perfectly true.

"The boy is right," Hector announced. "I do believe that we are stuck fast."

"Oh what a pity," Moravia said.

"Yes, bit of a shame that." Agamemnon added.

"Well what are you going to do?" Tomás asked.

"Hold a vote on it!" the rats announced in unison.

"Hold a vote?" Tomás exclaimed. "Hold a vote on it?"

"Oh yes, indeed," the rats replied. "Any decision that affects us all must be voted on."

"A simple majority is enough in most cases, but policy decisions must be ratified by a unanimous vote," Hector added.

The rats were about to disappear below to hold their vote when Tomás spoke: "I have a better idea," he said. "Why don't you rats turn the wheels in reverse and I shall push you off. I think that between us we should manage it easily."

The rats paused. "What do you think, Agamemnon old man?" Hector asked.

"It does seem a reasonable idea to me, Agamemnon," agreed Moravia.

"Put it to the vote then. All those members in favour say 'Aye'."

"Aye!" they chorused.

"Very well, young man." Agamemnon announced. "We shall do as you ask. Now then, Moravia, and you, Hector, if you would be so kind as to take up your positions and wait for this fine young man to give the signal."

Moravia and Hector took up their positions in their wheels, and Tomás waded over to the bow and put his shoulder to it. "Now!" he shouted.

Almost immediately Hector and Moravia began to run in their wheels and the paddles started to turn, throwing up great columns of turquoise water. Tomás pushed. Nothing happened at first but gently, the boat gradually started to move, slipping off the sand on which it had been stuck. At last it was free, sliding smoothly into deeper water. The rats stopped running and were soon scampering about on deck congratulating each other and squeaking happily.

"What about us?" Tomás called out, feeling rather annoyed with the rats.

"Ah, well, yes indeed," Hector spluttered. "You had better get on board. We can hardly leave for the Springtime without you, can we?"

Despite all the questions that were bubbling up in his mind, Tomás said nothing. Picking up Don Alfonso from the shore he waded out to the boat and placed him gently on to the deck. Then, with the last of his strength, he heaved himself on board and lay there.

"Let's get under way," Agamemnon said.

"Righty ho!" the other two agreed, taking up their positions in their wheels.

"Off we go!"

Hector and Moravia started running in their wheels once more while Agamemnon swung on the tiller bar, as the little green craft headed out into the wide turquoise stillness beneath the beige clouds and the yellow sky.

Don Alfonso curled up in the bows while Tomás sat on the deck watching as they pulled away from the shore. There was too much excitement on board the boat for anyone to have heard the clattering noise as the Wild Weaver lowered the bucket into the well once more.

"And what do they call you?" Agamemnon asked Tomás. "You must forgive me for not asking sooner."

"My name is Tomás, and this is Don Alfonso," he replied, pointing to his friend.

"Don Alfonso de Albaricoque y Dos Limones, if you please, Tomás," Don Alfonso added self-importantly.

"A real Spanish grandee!" Moravia exclaimed. "Oh, how much I admire the nobility."

"Oh yes," agreed Hector. "It is so rarely that one meets true quality."

Tomás laughed. "He's not a noble, he's only a dog!"

Don Alfonso looked hurt. "I'll have you know, young Tomás, that I come from a long line of grandees."

"Oh clearly," Agamemnon applauded. "Anyone can see it."

"Can they?" Tomás asked.

"Nobility is in the heart," Hector said, "not in the clothes. Who do you suppose said that?"

"The Learned Pibroch Rat," the others replied in unison.

"Who's the Learned Pibroch Rat?" Tomás asked.

"You have never heard of the Learned Pibroch Rat!" the rats exclaimed in surprise.

"Perhaps I may offer a little enlightenment to my friend," Don Alfonso suggested. "The Learned Pibroch Rat is the wisest of all rats. All his sayings are written down in, correct me if I am wrong, a chapter of the Great Law entitled 'Axioms and Sayings of The Learned Pibroch Rat'."

"Exactly!" Agamemnon agreed.

The shoreline was, by this time, little more than a dark smudge against the yellow and beige of the sky. Tomás was tired, hungry, confused and worse, he was still wet from his efforts in pushing the boat off the sand. Ahead of them lay the horizon, a thin, black line that divided the colours of the sky from the perfect turquoise stillness of the lake. He looked about him. Don Alfonso had curled up once more in the bows, Moravia and Hector were running easily in their wheels, while Agamemnon steered an almost straight course. The paddle wheels turned, churning up the water with a rush and a hiss as they bowled along.

As they sailed on, Tomás began to notice that there was no change in the light. Time must be passing, but there was no sign of night, just the same soft light everywhere that gave a gentle, comfortable glow. He shifted position until he was sitting by Don Alfonso.

"Where are we?" he asked softly.

"The Great Subterranean Lake, of course," came the reply.

Don Alfonso was about to say more when Agamemnon called out from the helm: "I think that we have gone far enough for now, and we could all do with a little rest."

"Hear, hear!" Hector agreed.

"Absolutely!" Moravia added.

No sooner had she spoken than both rats stopped running and climbed out on to the deck. Agamemnon slipped a bolt into the tiller to stop it moving and joined the others. Tomás and Don Alfonso watched.

"Gather round," Agamemnon ordered fussily.

"Gather round, you two gentlemen as well," indicating to his passengers to join the others beside him. "Good," he said. "Now, we shall have something to eat. Guests first."

Tomás looked at Don Alfonso. "What is there?" he asked shyly.

"What do you want?" Agamemnon replied.

"Do you have any sardines?"

"Certainly. How would you like them?"

"You mean that you can give me a plateful of sardines?"

"Indeed, young man. Now, how do you want them: raw, filletted, chopped, marinated in garlic butter, or fried in olive oil?"

Tomás thought for a moment, not quite sure that he believed what he was hearing. So many strange things had happened to him so far that he felt it must be true, but like most humans he was unable to accept what *is*. "Can you do them in oil with a little lettuce and tomato, and some bread?"

"At last," Agamemnon sighed. "Now, Don Alfonso, what about you?"

"Some jugged hare with some spring water, if you would be so kind."

"Very well."

Moravia and Hector added their orders and Agamemnon scuttled off below decks. There followed a crashing and banging of pans, the sound of knives chopping and slicing, followed by sizzling and frying. Very soon the smell of cooking was wafted up making Tomás realize just how hungry he was.

Some time later the sizzling and frying stopped, and was followed by more clattering and banging until Agamemnon finally emerged balancing a large plate of fried sardines on his head, and carrying the lettuce and bread in his paws. "Take it, take it," he urged Tomás. "The plate is hot and is burning the very fur on my head!"

Tomás needed no further asking. Taking the plate he immediately started to eat. Don Alfonso's jugged hare followed and, after another polite exchange, he too tucked into his meal. "As fine a jugged hare as I have ever tasted, Agamemnon old fellow, quite the best. You must give my compliments to the chef."

Agamemnon smiled through his whiskers. "It was nothing, dear Don Alfonso."

"These sardines are wonderful, Agamemnon," Tomás said, wiping up the last of the olive oil with his bread.

"We are here to oblige, dear boy," Agamemnon demurred.

"How did you do it?"

"How did I do what?"

"The sardines; how did you do them?"

"As you told me. Did I forget anything?"

Tomás shook his head, "You don't understand. What I mean is ..."

Before he could finish, Moravia interrupted him.

"I think that I know what you mean, Tomás. You would like to know how we managed to find sardines in such a place as this. Well, let us say that they appeared thanks to the Law of the Learned Pibroch Rat. You needed them, so they came to you. Does that make sense?"

Tomás shook his head. "No," he replied honestly.

Don Alfonso groaned. "Tomás, you have the shortest memory. Think back to the Tree of Desire."

"Yes."

"What did I tell you then?"

"That all I had to do was think of what I needed and, if it was part of my Purpose, it would come to me."

"Exactly."

"You see, Tomás," Hector said, "if you follow the Law of the Learned Pibroch Rat all these things become clear."

"The Law of the Learned Pibroch Rat," the other rats squealed together.

"I'm afraid that humans know nothing of the Pibroch Rat," Don Alfonso told them.

"Oh dear," said Hector.

"What a pity," echoed Moravia.

"Dearie me," added Agamemnon.

"You see, humans live by other laws, not those that we animals live by. That is why so few humans make this journey," Don Alfonso continued.

"But the Law of the Learned Pibroch Rat *is* the Law!" the rats exclaimed.

"Yes, but humans don't know it. They did once, but now ... well, they think that they are all powerful and have no need of the Law of the Learned Pibroch Rat."

"What a shame!" the rats responded sadly.

"Never mind," Moravia announced cheerfully. "I'm sure that Tomás can learn. You would like to learn the Law of the Learned Pibroch Rat, wouldn't you, Tomás?"

"I suppose so. But everything is so strange, I don't know if I can."

"Come along, Tomás," Don Alfonso assured him. "You have been learning ever since we started out, and you will know it well by the time we reach the Moon."

Agamemnon paused, sniffing the air through his little black nose and twitching his whiskers. "I think that we should be under way again. Might I ask you to take up your positions once more."

"Can you sense an outlet?" Hector enquired.

"Oh yes," Moravia said. "It is really quite near."

"Well then, we must make haste," Agamemnon said as he scurried back to his tiller.

The others disappeared into their wheels and, very soon, the great red paddle wheels began to turn, churning up the tranquil, turquoise water.

Tomás looked round. He could see nothing, nor could he hear anything. But wait! What was that gurgling noise? Frantically he looked about him and there, some distance off the bows he saw what looked like a great swirl of angry water that thundered downwards into a great black hole.

"What is that?" he called out in alarm.

Agamemnon was struggling with his tiller, but managed to reply, "It's a river, or at least the start of one."

"A river?"

"Exactly, and if you don't hurry up and give me a little help, I fear that we shall soon all be sailing down it."

Tomás did as he was asked, and between them they managed to steer the little craft away from the great, gurgling whirlpool that was the birth of a great river, and which gradually disappeared astern as once more they sailed on towards the far horizon.

They had been sailing for a long time, and Tomás was feeling tired. Despite all his questions about Subterranean Lakes, Pibroch Rats and all the other things that swam in his head, Tomás could not prevent himself from falling asleep. He crawled up to the bow and, laying his head on a coil of rope, drifted off into a dreamless sleep.

Chapter Six

The Mighty Centre and
the Singing Caves

For Tomás, time ceased to exist as the boat sailed
on. Was it actually going anywhere? Nothing
seemed to change — the beige clouds sat in the
yellow sky; the still, turquoise surface of the lake
stretched out before them. All he could do was
watch and wait.

Tomás was becoming very bored with waiting
when, somewhere in the distance he heard a
crashing noise that sounded very much like a
waterfall. How could it be? There was no waterfall
to be seen but the distant crashing continued,
growing ever louder.

"Do you hear that, Don Alfonso?" he asked,
shaking the dog awake.

"Hear what?"

"That crashing noise."

Don Alfonso pricked up his ears and listened.
"You're right, Tomás. I wonder what that can be?

I suppose that our good friends the rats have everything under their control."

Tomás agreed, and decided it must only be his imagination. He looked at Agamemnon who was swinging lazily from the tiller bar while the other rats were running smoothly in their wheels. He shrugged his shoulders as Don Alfonso curled up once more to sleep.

Tomás sat down and, taking out his knife, prepared to clean it. As he did so, he became aware that the crashing noise was becoming even louder. He looked up from his work, but could still see nothing. Where was it coming from? He looked about him once more, straining his eyes to follow the horizon when he noticed, some distance off, an odd yellow mist from where the crashing noise seemed to be coming. He shook Don Alfonso once more. "What is it now?" the dog muttered irritably.

"Just look over there," Tomás said, pointing towards the yellow mist.

Don Alfonso sat up and, his eyes wide with horror, howled: "I'll be blowed, it's the Mighty Centre. It's the Mighty Centre! Quickly, we must change course or we are lost." He struggled to his feet and hobbled down the deck calling out to Agamemnon, warning him of the approaching danger.

Agamemnon scrambled up the deck and stood in the bows twitching his nose. Then, in panic, the rat began scurrying about the deck frantically calling out for help. Moravia and Hector stopped running in their wheels and joined Agamemnon on the deck.

"What are we to do?" they cried. "It's the Mighty Centre! We are all doomed."

Tomás couldn't understand what all the panic was about. He looked ahead and could see that the thundering yellow mist was even closer. He could see too that the mist was the foam thrown up by a vast cascade of water that seemed to fall out of the sky. "What is it?" he asked Don Alfonso in astonishment.

"The Mighty Centre; the very heart of it all," Don Alfonso replied, without turning his gaze from the cascade of water that was drawing closer with each passing moment.

"I don't understand."

Don Alfonso brushed him aside. "If we survive, I will tell you all about it. But now we must do something quickly."

As he spoke so the rats had gathered on the stern and were squeaking and chattering in despair.

"What are you lot up to?" Don Alfonso shouted.

"You know the Law of the Learned Pibroch Rat as well as we do," Hector replied. "You know what it says about rats and sinking ships."

"But we're not sinking." Don Alfonso replied crossly.

"We soon will be," Moravia answered glumly.

Don Alfonso shook his head and bared his teeth. "We are not going to sink, so there is no need for you to be the first to leave, is there?"

Agamemnon looked hard at the row of sharp, white teeth and replied hurriedly, "Well, old man, since you put it like that, perhaps we could delay our departure. Couldn't we?"

"Oh yes," the others agreed.

Don Alfonso smiled. "Good. Now this is what we are going to do," he announced, drawing the rats to him.

Tomás could only watch as Don Alfonso issued his instructions. The rats scampered about, falling over themselves to obey. Moravia and Hector clambered down into the starboard wheel while Agamemnon took up his position at the tiller. Don Alfonso then turned to Tomás. "Tie that rope round my waist, tightly now, it must not slip. I am going for a swim." he spoke quickly, glancing all the time at the ever nearing downrush of water. "Now, tie the other end to that ring on the bow, and then help Agamemnon on the tiller. Do you understand?"

Tomás caught up the rope, tied it securely round Don Alfonso's waist and quickly tied the other end to the iron ring on the deck. Satisfied that he was secure, Don Alfonso leaped into the water and started to swim. Tomás watched his friend bobbing away, pulling the rope tightly behind him. Sure that he could do no more, Tomás ran down the deck as quickly as he could to help Agamemnon on the tiller bar.

"Go!" Don Alfonso shouted once the rope was taut. He began swimming away from the waterfall with strong strokes, for though he might have moved with difficulty on land Don Alfonso was a superb swimmer. Hector and Moravia began running furiously in the starboard wheel while Agamemnon and Tomás pulled the tiller hard over.

At first nothing much happened and it seemed that nothing could save them from the Mighty Centre. Then, little by little, the bow started to answer, turning away from the cascade until, to everyone's relief, the little vessel was running alongside it. The spray drenched them all like a heavy rainstorm, but no one noticed until they finally began to pull away. Hector leapt from the starboard side and was soon running in his own wheel. Agamemnon straightened up the tiller while Tomás hurried to retrieve Don Alfonso from the water. As quickly as he could, the boy pulled in the rope, dragging the dripping dog back on to the deck where he collapsed in a panting heap.

The rats all cheered. Tomás cheered, too, looking back over the stern to watch as the Mighty Centre returned to a harmless spray in the distance.

"How are you, Don Alfonso?" Tomás asked his

friend, who was still panting on the deck, his long pink tongue lolling from the side of his mouth. He didn't answer at first but rose, unsteadily, to his feet and, shaking himself vigorously, replied, "That was a trifle more difficult than I thought it would be."

"What was going on?" Tomás asked.

"Perhaps I might be able to help, Tomás," Agamemnon called from the tiller. "I fear that dear Don Alfonso will need some time to rest from his exertions. What we came so close to being swallowed up by was, as you know, called the Mighty Centre.

As he carefully steered the fragile craft away from the plunging mass of water, which was by now only a yellow haze on the horizon once more, Agamemnon continued to explain: "Tomás, have you ever thought what happens to all the water that is sloshing round up there?"

Tomás looked upwards briefly, but could only see the beige clouds in the yellow sky. "I suppose it all soaks into the ground and that's it," he said.

"Aha!" Agamemnon exclaimed, "that's only the half of it. You see, when it rains on the surface the water collects and seeps deep into the ground, as you rightly say, but that is not all. From there it flows back to the Mighty Centre and crashes, as you have seen, back into the Great Subterranean Lake to begin its journey all over again — down the rivers of Spain to the sea, where it evaporates and is carried over the sierras once more as clouds, to fall on the Earth as rain. This, Tomás, is known as the Cycle of Life and is the first and most important chapter in the whole Law of the Learned Pibroch Rat. It is the only Law that we all obey whether or not we believe in it. Do you see?"

Tomás had to admit that he couldn't really.

Don Alfonso sat up and looked about him. "Tomás," he said. "Have you ever wondered what happens to all the rain that falls; why we aren't always wading about in water up to our bellies, all the time?"

"Because it all soaks down here in the way Agamemnon said?" he asked.

"Exactly. You humans don't know the half of it," Don Alfonso laughed.

"So where do we go now?" Tomás asked. "We can't pass through the Mighty Centre, can we?"

"There is only one place where we can bypass the Mighty Centre safely, and that is through the Singing Caves," Agamemnon told them, "but it is a very dangerous route; one false move and the Mighty Centre sinks you."

Tomás shook his head. "I would never have believed it if I hadn't seen it all with my own eyes," he said. "What happens after that?"

"You are learning the Law of the Learned Pibroch Rat," Agamemnon told him. "Slowly you will understand until the time comes when you will truly be ready to walk to the Moon. And after the Singing Caves ...?" he added lightly. "Well, we sail on to the Springtime."

"I don't think that I shall ever understand all this," Tomás admitted sadly. "It's all too much for me."

"You will, Tomás," Don Alfonso assured him gently. "You will."

Tomás hadn't noticed, but Agamemnon had altered course once more and they were now sailing parallel to the Mighty Centre, but at a safe distance from it. Once again everyone regained their calm, except for Tomás, who couldn't quite take his eyes off the seemingly endless plunging wall of water that thundered nearby.

On and on they sailed until, what appeared to be a shoreline came into view at last. "Is that it?" Don Alfonso asked Agamemnon.

The rat nodded his head. "We have to be very careful here," he said. "Do you see over there?" he pointed towards the rugged coastline with his tail.

Tomás and Don Alfonso strained their eyes as the coastline came closer. At last they could see some jagged rocks just off the bow, that poked dangerously from the water. Their little boat seemed to be heading directly for them and towards certain destruction when they suddenly felt the cold spray of the Mighty Centre raining down on them. They were trapped!

"Now," Agamemnon called out. "Do you see those rocks over there?"

"Yes," Tomás replied rather nervously. "But aren't we a bit close to the Mighty Centre?"

"Not while we stay on this course," Agamemnon told him. "Over there are the Singing Caves."

"Why are they called that?" Tomás asked.

"If you listen carefully, you may hear them above the noise of the water."

Tomás listened. At first he could only hear the crashing of the mighty waterfall, but gradually, as he listened more closely, he could just hear a low moaning. "Is that it?" he asked, pointing in the general direction of the sound.

"Yes," Agamemnon replied. "The moaning sound you can hear are the winds howling through the caves. We have to catch one of those winds to be taken through. That's the hard bit."

They travelled on. The water was becoming choppy now and the little green boat was bobbing up and down rather alarmingly. Hector and Moravia carried on running in their wheels as if there were nothing more natural than the dark, ragged, rocky coast in front of them. With the Mighty Centre crashing down to their left and the ragged rocks on their right waiting for any mistake, Tomás felt nervous, and Don Alfonso certainly looked it. Onwards they sailed with the water becoming rougher by the moment and the dangers ever closer. However, none of the rats looked particularly bothered. In fact, Agamemnon, was nonchalantly leaning against the tiller bar and preening his magnificent whiskers. Then, all of a sudden, he tensed and grasped the tiller tightly in both paws. As he did so Hector and Moravia leapt from their wheels.

"Here she comes," they shouted.

Before either Tomás or Don Alfonso could say anything, they were overtaken by a low moaning sound that seemed to grow louder and louder until it was howling directly above them. The wind caught up the little boat as if it were an autumn leaf and whirled it over the wild water. Almost at once, they were carried into a long cave. "Hang on tightly!" Agamemnon managed to shout above the noise, just before they disappeared from the light.

Through the caves the wind carried them, while it moaned sadly in the surrounding darkness until, suddenly, they were shot out into the light, like a cork from a bottle, landing with a mighty splash on the tranquil, turquoise surface of the Great Subterranean Lake once more.

Tomás caught his breath and noticed that the Mighty Centre was still there, but they were now bobbing away from it. Hector and Moravia resumed their places in the wheel and Agamemnon took up his position once more on the tiller. "I told you there was nothing to worry about," he announced confidently.

As they pulled steadily away from the Singing Caves and all the dangers that surrounded them, Tomás felt that he could relax. Don Alfonso was sitting alongside Agamemnon who, with barely a twitch of his whiskers, lolled on the tiller post while maintaining a generally straight course towards the horizon. Tomás joined them. "Why do you suppose that human people have never heard of the Law of the Learned Pibroch Rat?" he asked.

"No idea," Agamemnon admitted.

Don Alfonso scratched himself before speaking. "It's not that human people don't heed the Law of the Great Pibroch Rat, it's just that when they do they call it something else, something more appropriate to human people, like 'poetry' for example."

Tomás looked confused. He had heard poets; every mulero that put up at La Peña fancied himself a poet. When he had a moment he would often steal into the courtyard and listen at the window while they told the fantastic tales of their journeys across Spain. "Poetry is just fantastic stories, isn't it?" he asked.

"Stories are only fantastic when you don't believe them," Don Alfonso said. "These stories, poems you call them, or songs, contain some of the Law of the Learned Pibroch Rat. Sadly, this is all that you have left. You see, we animal people still have the Law, and that is why we make this journey."

"Where did it come from?" Tomás asked. He thought it very unfair that humans had not heard the Law of the Learned Pibroch Rat, and wondered why the animals kept it to themselves.

"Let me answer that," Agamemnon said. "A long, long time ago, when the world was young and there was nothing but the four winds and the sierras, there appeared on the Earth two very special creatures — a sparrow and a rat. Now there was a very good reason for this. The sparrow was charged with finding the missing note that would set the universe back on its correct course, and the rat was to guide everything else in the ways of the universe. He was called Pibroch because that was what he wrote."

"And where is this Pibroch thing?" Tomás asked.

"At the very end of the earthly part of our journey Tomás," Don Alfonso told him. *The Great Book of the Learned Pibroch Rat,* as it is known, is kept by La Madre. La Madre, or the Mother, is the last signpost on our way. We have to find her for it is she who decides whether or not we can go on to the Moon."

"So this journey is really a way of learning the Law of the Learned Pibroch Rat?"

"Yes," Don Alfonso agreed. "You have already learned a great deal, Tomás, but there is a great deal more too."

"What happens next?"

Don Alfonso howled. "Tomás, you never stop asking questions. What happens next is that we arrive at the Springtime on the other side of the Great Subterranean Lake."

"And we should soon be there," Agamemnon told them.

This news filled Tomás with expectation. So many unbelievable things had happened to him that he wondered what other wonderful things lay ahead. He lay down on the deck and watched the beige clouds as they drifted in the yellow sky, and thought about the sparrow and the Pibroch Rat until his head began to ache.

Chapter Seven

The Riddle of the Nunnapooses

He was just becoming bored again with the seemingly endless journey across the Subterranean
Lake when, looking towards the horizon from
the bows, Tomás felt sure that he could make out
a coastline. It seemed, at first, to be a trick of
the light. After all, he had been staring at the
horizon for a long time and was tired, but as time
passed, and they drew closer, it became clear that
what he could see was indeed a coastline. Soon,
he could make out mountain ranges that rose out
of the turquoise water and stood silent and
black against the yellow sky. The closer they
sailed, the clearer features became until he
could pick out individual rocks. Agamemnon
steered the vessel so they were travelling along
the coast until, eventually, they reached a headland, similar in shape to the one that they had
left so long ago. There was one big difference
however — the shore that they had left was green
and carpeted with a wonderful array of flowers,

but this coast was bare and rather forbidding. It seemed lifeless.

"Where are we?" Tomás called out.

Don Alfonso hobbled up the deck as quickly as he could, panting nervously; "You must be quiet here, Tomás, for this is the realm of the Nunnapooses," he whispered.

"The Nunnapooses?"

"I beg of you, Tomás, please be quiet. We are in grave danger if the Nunnapooses show up."

Tomás turned round and saw Agamemnon fiddling nervously with his whiskers while Hector and Moravia ran slowly in their wheels, with the greatest care.

Gradually, they edged round the headland and entered a broad, sandy bay. Here the sheer rock face rose abruptly from a thin strip of yellow sand. About half way along, Tomás could see a series of steps cut into the black rock, that led up to what appeared to be the mouth of a cave.

Skilfully, Agamemnon steered the tiny vessel until it brushed the shoaling sand and came to a halt. It was quite a different arrival from their first appearance on the far shore. With quick, fearful steps Agamemnon left the tiller and made his way to the bow from where he glanced into the water. Then he beckoned to Tomás and Don Alfonso indicating that they should join him. "We've arrived," he whispered. "You must go now. Climb up those stairs and go through the doorway, I cannot tell you more. Only remember the Pibroch Rat and be careful. We must leave now for the Nunnapooses have little time for us rats." He took Tomás' hand in his paws and shook it vigorously. "You are a good boy, Tomás. I know that you will make it." Then he turned to Don Alfonso. "Perhaps we shall meet again, old chap," he said. "Perhaps one day soon Moravia, Hector and myself will follow you."

"It's been a pleasure, my dear fellow," Don Alfonso replied warmly. "A great honour it has been for both of us."

"Quickly now, you must go," Hector hissed.

"Good Luck and remember the Law," Moravia added softly.

Agamemnon took up the rope from the bow and lowered it silently into the water, indicating as he did so that Tomás and Don Alfonso should climb down it.

It was only a short distance, so Tomás was able to pick up Don Alfonso quite easily and carry him into the water which, to his surprise, barely reached his knees. Lowering his friend gently on to the beach, Tomás returned to the boat to help push it back out to sea. In almost total silence he heaved as Hector and Moravia scrambled desperately in their wheels until, with a slight sucking noise, the craft slipped out into deeper water.

Tomás rejoined Don Alfonso on the beach where they sat and watched the little green boat, with its huge red paddle wheels, sail out of the bay, disappearing back round the headland, leaving them alone once more on a strange and forbidding coast.

It took both Tomás and Don Alfonso a little time to appreciate just where they were. There was total silence. Both friends felt uncertain and afraid of being alone as they looked about them. There was the ominous staircase that led upwards to a doorway, and then to who knew where?

Don Alfonso sat up and scratched himself. "We had better be on our way," he said. "We can't just stay here."

"What about the Nunnapooses?" Tomás asked.

Don Alfonso shook his head and led the way to the stairway. "What about them? We have to carry on I fear; there is no way out of here but through that tunnel. You had better carry me up," he suggested.

Without another word, Tomás did as he was asked, and very soon they stood at the entrance to a long, dark passageway that led deep into the rock face. There was no light or sound to help them, just what seemed like eternal darkness.

"What are we to do, Don Alfonso?" Tomás whispered nervously.

"I don't think we have much choice," Don Alfonso replied softly. "If you lead, you can feel your way with your hands. This passage must lead somewhere."

Fearfully, Tomás did as he was asked. Slowly, carefully, he edged along the tunnel with Don Alfonso hobbling close behind. Once his eyes became used to the blackness that enveloped them, Tomás grew in confidence. The walls of the tunnel were surprisingly smooth, while the floor seemed to be covered with what felt like soft sand. There was no sound, but both boy and dog became aware of a smell that grew stronger the further they moved along the passageway. It was a strange smell. Tomás immediately thought of Fat Francisco's goats while Don Alfonso, who had an idea of what might be causing it, felt sure that it must be the Nunnapooses, but decided that it was probably better not to say anything.

The deeper they edged down the tunnel, the stronger and more unpleasant the smell became. Tomás stopped and peered ahead of him. Was that a light ahead? He could just make out two pinpoints of green light in the distance that appeared to flicker on and off. He knelt down and, putting his lips to Don Alfonso's ear, whispered, "Do you see those lights?"

The dog nodded. "Thankfully there's only one of them."

"Only one of what?"

"Those lights are cat's eyes. There is a Nunna-poose down there waiting for us."

"A cat, is that all?" Tomás laughed scornfully.

"Be quiet, Tomás please!" Don Alfonso hissed.

"These are not the cats that you know. These are the dreaded Nunnapooses."

As he spoke, so the first green eyes were joined by another pair. "What are we to do?" Tomás asked.

"Now that they know that we are here, I suppose we had better keep going. But be careful."

So they carried on, slowly edging their way down the tunnel. As they did so, so the eyes became larger, the smell became stronger, and they could soon detect the sound of cats purring. Suddenly, the eyes disappeared and the purring stopped leaving the travellers to grope their way unaided.

At last, the tunnel began to broaden and open out, until they turned a sharp corner to discover a dimly lit cavern ahead of them. The smell, by this time, was unbelievable. However, the very idea of light cheered Tomás up — that was, until he saw huge mountains of animal bones before him, piled up almost to the jagged roof. There were bones of all shapes and sizes: leg bones, wing bones, rib cages, round bones, flat bones. In fact, an example of almost every bone imaginable.

He looked about him in horror, for perched on ledges around the cavern were innumerable skulls; skulls of many travellers along this road, and skulls of the lost, in which dim lights now burned and gave the whole scene a ghostly feel. To his great relief, the boy noticed that at the furthest end of the gruesome cavern there was a splendid, sweeping staircase which led away from the ghastly bone-littered hall.

"Quickly!" Tomás shouted, pointing to the staircase. "Let's run for it."

They were just about to make a dash between the piles of bones to escape up the staircase, when a huge tabby cat sprang from behind one of the rotting piles.

"There's one 'Poose," Don Alfonso observed dryly, when from behind a pile of assorted rib cages sprang another, equally fearsome, tabby. Don Alfonso turned round and bared his teeth, "And there's a Nunna' one!"

Tomás picked up a large bone from the nearest pile and waved it above his head threateningly.

The first Nunnapoose simply curled up in front of them, blocking their route to the staircase, and began to purr, while the Nunnapoose behind started stretching, exposing his long, sharp claws as he did so. Don Alfonso growled.

"Welcome," the first Nunnapoose purred, smiling broadly. "Welcome to our humble lair."

"Let us pass!" Tomás shouted.

The Nunnapoose licked her lips. "Did you hear that?" she called out to her partner. "They want to leave."

The other continued stretching and baring his claws. "How disappointing," he smiled.

"Let us pass!" Tomás shouted once more, his voice echoing round the dismal cavern.

"Not so fast, young man," the first Nunnapoose said. "You can't just arrive somewhere and not stay awhile without causing great offence."

"Grrrreat offence," added the other.

"We didn't ask to come here," Tomás replied angrily.

"Then why are you here, young man?" the Nunnapoose asked sweetly.

Tomás thought for a moment and fell silent.

"That's better," she said. "You have to watch your manners when you are someone's guest."

"Much better," agreed her partner. "It's just as well that we are so broad-minded otherwise something nasty might have happened."

"What do you want from us?" Don Alfonso asked.

The Nunnapooses both smiled. "Just a little help with our puzzle, that's all," they said.

"We have been trying for such a long time to work out this problem, and nobody has yet been able to help us."

"What happened to them?" Tomás asked fearfully.

The first Nunnapoose looked about her and purred wickedly. "They stayed behind to help us."

Tomás waved his arm, taking in the huge piles of bones that littered the great cavern. "I suppose that these are the others?" he asked.

"Purrfectly correct," the other smirked.

Tomás raised the bone above his head, and advanced towards the Nunnapoose who merely exposed her claws. "You haven't heard what the problem is yet," she told him matter of factly.

"Tell them," the other called.

"Very well. Listen carefully to what I tell you and if you answer correctly then you may go, but if you cannot, well then, you must stay and help us until we find the answer."

The Nunnapoose began to sing, in her cat-like way:

> There is one small thing
> That could make our hearts sing.
> It is something long sought,
> That we hope you have brought.
> Really not much to ask;
> Such a convenient task!
> A task, surely, that ought
> To be considered as nought.
> So where is it, this thing
> That we asked you to bring?

The Nunnapoose finished her little rhyme and purred: "I'm waiting."

"We're waiting," the other added, sharpening his claws threateningly.

"What are we to do?" Tomás asked Don Alfonso hurriedly.

"I'm just trying to remember what Gabri told me."

Tomás looked about him, the Nunnapooses were growing restless. "Did Gabri tell you to expect this?"

"In a manner of speaking. We were sitting round the old shepherd's fire one night, somewhere in the Sierra Morena, when he told me. Now what was it?"

"Quickly!" Tomás urged, feeling, as he did so, for his knife. As his hand moved in his pocket, to his surprise he felt something large, like a ball; a large ball that had certainly not been there before. Quickly, he took it out, and was astonished to find a large ball of string in his hand.

"That's it!" Don Alfonso exclaimed with delight. "A ball of string! It fits the rhyme. Don't you see? Now throw it."

"Where?"

"Anywhere but at the staircase!"

Mustering all his strength, the boy hurled the ball of string in the direction from which they had come.

With one mighty bound, the first Nunnapoose leapt over them and took off in pursuit of the rapidly unravelling string, quickly followed by her partner. In an instant, both Nunnapooses had disappeared into the gloom, lost amongst the piles of rotting bones.

"Run for it!" Don Alfonso shouted, leading the

way. Without looking one way or the other, they flew up the magnificent staircase and out of that dreadful place.

Blindly they ran, crashing into the tunnel walls in their rush to escape the Nunnapooses until, at long last, the tunnel appeared to turn upwards. Don Alfonso stopped. "I think we are safe now," he panted.

Tomás dropped to his knees. He was exhausted and wanted nothing better than to stop. "Are we safe?" he gasped.

"Yes," Don Alfonso replied. "I don't think there is much further to go now. So let's wait here for a moment."

Tomás froze. "Don Alfonso," he hissed. "Did you hear that?"

"What?"

"That noise just then. It sounded like somebody following us."

Don Alfonso laughed. "How could anybody be following us?"

"What about the Nunnapooses?"

"Oh, they're much too busy playing with your ball of string to worry about us. No, it's your imagination."

Tomás was not convinced. He strained every muscle to listen, but all he could hear was the silence that surrounded them.

"Perhaps you're right," he agreed.

"Let's wait here for a little while to catch our

breath," Don Alfonso suggested. "I fear that my leg is paying the price for our escape."

Tomás sat down and rested against the wall of the tunnel. He too was tired. "What happens next?" he asked shortly.

"We carry on until we come out in the Spring-time," Don Alfonso replied.

"How do you mean?"

"Spring, Tomás! Spring! You like the Spring-time, don't you?"

"Oh yes!" he agreed enthusiastically.

"And you don't like winter?"

"Not much." Tomás remembered his little room behind La Peña, and how cold it was when the north wind blew across the city from the snow-covered peaks of the Sierra Nevada.

"One of the reasons why we travelled the Great Subterranean Lake was to avoid having to journey from the south through the winter snows to the high Guadarramas. Not a very pleasant experience, I can tell you," Don Alfonso told him while licking his injured leg. "Why, I re-member a time, many years ago now when Gabri, me, Hercules, the Pyrenean and little Porro were lost in a snowstorm in the Sierra Morena, while looking for stray sheep. For days we wandered about until Gabri found the shep-herd's hut once more and we were saved. No, it is much better to travel underground during the winter."

"Why have we come to the Guadarramas, though?"

"Because it's on our way I suppose. Now then, if you are quite rested, I think that we should get going. It's no good sitting here."

Aching in every bone, Tomás stood up and followed Don Alfonso who, despite his injured leg, hobbled along at quite a brisk pace.

The tunnel rose easily at first, but the further they went, the steeper the climb became and both boy and dog were soon finding the climb increasingly difficult. Just when it seemed that the tunnel would never end, their attention was drawn to a distant speck of daylight ahead. The sight of real daylight after so long below ground gave them new energy, and with one more effort they struggled towards the light until, at last, they tumbled out on to a rocky mountainside.

Chapter Eight

The Gitanillo's Bargain

Blinking in the bright sunlight, Tomás and Don Alfonso sat for a moment to take in their surroundings, and to plan their next move. They looked about them at the jagged, snowcapped peaks of the beautiful Sierra Guadarrama. All around them they could hear the familiar call of the birds as they soared in the warm, blue sky. Torrents of melting snow tumbled down the rocky slopes, running into deep, cold lakes that shone brightly far below. Tomás breathed deeply, taking in the familiar smell of the sierras; the delicate fragrance of thyme and lavender mingled with the fresh tang of pine. He was pleased to be free of the tunnel and once more in a world that he could understand.

"So where are we?" Tomás asked as he surveyed the high peaks on the distant horizon.

"How do you mean?" Don Alfonso replied as he stretched.

"How much further do we have to go?"

Don Alfonso scratched himself, as he often did when thinking. "Well, if I can remember properly all that Gabri told me, we just have to find the Red Bull who will take us to the Mother of All, and that's it."

"What do you mean?"

"I mean, Tomás, that I have no idea what happens after the Mother. She is, as far as I know, the last stop between here and the Moon."

"Is this Mother the same one that you told me about?" Tomás asked.

"She's the same, all right. She keeps the Book."

"The Law of the Learned Pibroch Rat?"

"Yes."

"Is it far?"

Don Alfonso shook his head. "I really have no idea. All Gabri told me was that we would find her, and she would tell us what to do. You see, the Mother knows everything: she is everything."

"I don't understand."

Don Alfonso howled. "Tomás, why oh why can't you just accept what *is* and what is not. The Mother is *the* Mother — the Mother of everything."

"But Don Alfonso ..." Tomás' voice trailed away. "Do you still think that we can make it?" he asked softly.

"Of course we will."

Tomás gave his friend a hug. "I couldn't go on without you," he said.

Don Alfonso responded with a wet lick. "We won't get very far sitting here. Look, the sun is getting higher and hotter. We'd better be on our way."

Tomás was just about to ask another question when Don Alfonso suddenly pricked up his ears. "Did you hear that?" he hissed.

"No, but ..."

"There it is again. Follow me and be quiet." So saying, Don Alfonso hobbled off across the slope with Tomás hurrying behind, towards a large grey rock that stood alone amongst some thick, tussocky grass a short distance away .

He stopped again and cocked his ears once more. "You must have heard that?" he whispered urgently.

Tomás strained his ears but could hear nothing other than the wind. Then, just as he was about to tell Don Alfonso as much, he heard a faint voice calling out from a clump of grass a short distance beyond the rock. "Help!" it cried.

"Someone's in trouble," Tomás suggested, pointing in the direction of the voice.

"It's a Gitanillo," Don Alfonso replied seriously. "I knew it as soon as I heard the voice."

Tomás laughed. "Gitanillos aren't real," he replied confidently.

"Help!" the little voice cried out again.

"There isn't time to explain to you, Tomás." Don Alfonso told him sharply. "You must run over there as quickly as you can, and when I tell you, grab hold of the Gitanillo by his belt. No matter what he tries to do, do not let go of him! Do you understand?"

Tomás nodded and ran helter-skelter towards the voice. To his surprise he arrived to find a little man in a brightly coloured gypsy costume, trapped up to his waist in a rabbit hole.

"Help me!" the Gitanillo cried as he struggled to free himself from the hole, but his efforts only succeeded in sinking him deeper.

Without saying a word, Tomás took hold of the little man's arms and pulled. At first he wouldn't budge, but the more the boy pulled, so the Gitanillo was gradually able to work his way free of the hole.

"Grab hold of his belt!" Don Alfonso shouted, "and keep a tight hold!"

Tomás was just in time, for no sooner had the Gitanillo freed himself than he tried to escape, but the boy held him tight by his broad, black leather belt.

"Don't give him a chance to escape, Tomás," Don Alfonso said, as he carefully approached the struggling Gitanillo. "Now then, my fine friend," he continued, addressing himself to the little man who was kicking and punching at Tomás to free himself. "We have saved your life and we demand the bargain."

The Gitanillo stopped struggling and scowled.

"Fair enough," he replied gruffly. "What do you want?"

"Let him go," Don Alfonso ordered.

Tomás did as he was told but watched the Gitanillo carefully just in case he tried to escape.

"We have to find the Red Bull of Bailén and you will help us," Don Alfonso told him.

"You have saved my life, dog, and you have made the bargain. I will help you," the little man agreed. "From this rock, you must walk the whole summer long. Be sure to keep the rising sun to your left, and the setting sun to your right. Make sure that the blue mountains are before you, and you will surely find the Red Bull. You have a long way to go but the Gitanillo will help you. That is the bargain." Then he was gone, scampering off down the slope until he disappeared among some pine trees.

"What was all that about?" Tomás asked in amazement.

"You've heard of the Gitanillos, I suppose?"

Tomás nodded.

"And did no one tell you what to do if you ever found one?"

Tomás laughed. "They said that if you ever caught a Gitanillo then he had to grant you any wish you wanted, in return for letting him go. But that was just an old wives' tale!"

"Was it?" Don Alfonso asked. "I have heard much truth from old wives. Tomás, you must not dismiss something because you cannot believe it. There are many strange and wonderful things in the world that we must never close our minds to."

"I suppose so," the boy agreed. "So what do we do now?"

"We do as the Gitanillo told us. See the setting sun over there? We must keep that on our right-hand side, and those mountains in front of us. Now, let's go." With that, Don Alfonso hobbled along a little path that led away from the peak and down into the valley below. Before them lay the summer-scorched interior of Spain and, somewhere out there, the Red Bull of Bailén.

As the Gitanillo had told them, this part of their journey was the longest and the most difficult. Day after day, beneath the blazing summer sun, they crossed those flat, scorched and empty tablelands, which were red like dried blood beneath their feet. The flatlands, in turn, gave way to the grey and brown sierras, which rose to a faint blue where they seemed to touch the sky. All summer long, Tomás and Don Alfonso trudged along their weary road. Each day saw them rise with the sun and walk until it became too hot, when they were forced to seek out some shelter in which to sleep away the afternoon.

The walk would have been impossible but for the help of the Gitanillos. To their constant surprise, cool water would appear when they were thirsty, and food when they were hungry. There was always shelter from the heat and somewhere safe to rest for the night but, most importantly, their way was always pointed out to them, for though no Gitanillo was ever seen, their presence was always felt. However, Tomás felt certain that there was some other presence with them; something powerful, but gentle and caring besides. He mentioned this to Don Alfonso who always blamed his imagination or the heat, and waved away his fears with a casual flick of his injured paw.

One night in early autumn, when the heat of the day had turned to a damp chill and the stars twinkled more brightly in the night sky, the footsore travellers arrived at the mouth of a cave high on the side of a wild southern sierra. As was now customary, they found some bread and cheese laid out for them, as well as a string of spicy chorizo sausage and a large pot of cool, clear spring water for them to drink. As night fell, Tomás cut some dry rosemary and collected some wood from which he was able to make a fire to keep them warm.

They had just finished eating, and were silently gazing up at the beautiful autumn Moon as it rose into the sky above the jagged peaks, when their peace was disturbed by a dreadful pounding noise that echoed around the mountains. The noise became deafening until at last it faded away, far away on the silent plain that lay below where they were sitting.

"What was that?" Tomás asked fearfully.

"The Bull probably," Don Alfonso replied in his infuriatingly matter of fact way.

"The Red Bull of Bailén?"

"Possibly. I expect he's just returned home from a hard day's pawing and snorting."

Tomás sat in awed silence for some moments. "He must be a very large bull," he said at last.

Don Alfonso laughed, "Now you wouldn't be expecting the Red Bull of Bailén to be a scrawny calf or something, would you?" he said.

Tomás agreed that he wouldn't but added that he had never heard a noise like that before.

Don Alfonso stretched himself out before the fire, yawned and began to speak, "I remember once, a long time ago in the Sierra de Bermejas as I recall. Gabri and me were sitting round the shepherd's campfire. I think that little Porro was there, and one or two others, when Hercules the Pyrenean asked Gabri which was the strongest animal in all of Spain. Without hesitation Gabri replied, that it could only be the Red Bull of Bailén. He told us about his long horns of pure silver, his hooves of glowing brass, and how he could snort fire if he put his mind to it."

Tomás interrupted, laughing, "This is just one of your stories, isn't it?"

"No, no, every word is true. I'm telling you that this Red Bull of Bailén is not to be taken lightly," Don Alfonso replied earnestly.

"You said that he is going to take us to the Mother," Tomás reminded him.

"And so he will. Don't ask me how, but that's his Purpose," he added reassuringly.

This reassurance was of little comfort to the boy who, later that night, lay beside the remains of the fire unable to sleep, thinking only of what might happen when they met the fearsome Red Bull of Bailén. Tomorrow perhaps?

The next day dawned bright and almost clear. The autumn rains had yet to fall, but the air that morning was cool and damp which is a sure sign in that part of the world that it is about to rain.

Don Alfonso stirred first for it was at this time of year that his injured leg became particularly stiff, and was always sore when he woke up. How often had he cursed his ill luck but, looking down at the sleeping figure of Tomás beside the fire, he was pleased now that he had such a friend. It amazed Don Alfonso how things seemed to work out when you don't try to force them.

He breathed the new day in deeply and enjoyed the stillness of that quiet time for a few moments before gently nudging Tomás awake.

Tomás, to Don Alfonso's surprise, leapt from the ground shouting wildly: "Where's the Bull! Quick, the Bull's coming."

"No, no, it's only me," Don Alfonso told him gently. "There's no Bull. Here, I've saved you some chorizo and bread."

Gratefully, Tomás took the sausage and bread and started to eat while Don Alfonso looked about outside for signs of their path.

He returned some time later with the news that he had found a way down to the plain below. The dawn was breaking all around them, and a clear, fresh wind blew keenly making their progress brisk.

A narrow, twisting path led them down the mountainside and on to the dusty plain below. As they walked, so they became aware of a loud roaring noise, that sounded very much like snoring. The further they walked, the louder the noise became until its rising and falling drowned out even the chirping of the birds. Fearfully, almost on tiptoes, Tomás and Don Alfonso made their way towards the noise until, at last, they came to the mouth of a massive cave in the side of the very mountain down which they had just scrambled. There, fast asleep and snoring heavily, lay none other than the Red Bull of Bailén, his huge body rising and falling with each noisy breath. As they approached, so a single, brown, bloodshot eye slowly opened

Chapter Nine

The Red Bull of Bailén

After a few moments the massive head rose, and Tomás could see the magnificent sweep of the Bull's silver horns shining brightly in the sunlight,.

The Bull yawned and struggled to his feet, shaking off the dust that the night breeze had sprinkled upon him. "Good morning to you," he said, pawing the ground with his huge brass-shod hooves.

"Morning, Bull," Don Alfonso replied cheerfully as if he were greeting an old friend.

The Bull blinked and stopped pawing. "Blimey!" he exclaimed. "If it's not my old chum Don ... Hang on a moment ... Don Eduardo. No, he was darker. Don't tell me, I've always had a good memory for faces. Now, let me see. There was a dog just like you that I met once somewhere over there where the sun sets. Don ..., wait a moment, Don ..."

"Alfonso," Don Alfonso prompted.

The Bull let out a great bass laugh that echoed round the mountains and made the rocks rumble. "Don Alfonso de Albaricoque y Dos Limones, of course. My dear fellow, how are you? What a jolly fine surprise, you turning up here. You should have written."

"No time, Bull old thing," Don Alfonso replied breezily. "Me and the shaver here are walking to the Moon."

Tomás, amazed by this exchange of pleasantries, allowed himself to be pushed forward by Don Alfonso until he stood before the gigantic frame of the Red Bull of Bailén. "This is my friend Tomás, Bull old man. We've come all this way to see you."

"Nice to know you, young feller," the Bull said. "So you're walking to the Moon as well?"

Tomás swallowed hard. "Yes, sir," he managed to whisper.

"Cat got yer tongue, me laddo?" the Bull asked, roaring once more with laughter and making Tomás blush. "Sorry about that, youngster, but Don Felipe there will tell you what I am like. Eh! Now then, how can I help?"

"Gabri said that you would take us to see the Mother," Tomás suggested.

The Bull roared with laughter once more. "The Mother, eh? And why should you want to see her?"

"Because it's our Purpose to go and your Purpose to take us," Tomás replied, a little impatiently.

124

This only caused the huge Bull to laugh even more. "I'll tell you what, Don Carlos ..."

"Alfonso!" Don Alfonso reminded him.

"Alfonso, begging yours, old man, but this lad's got a bit of fire in his belly, don'tcha know."

"He's a good lad, Bull," Don Alfonso assured him.

"Oh yes, I can see that," the Bull replied, before turning his attention to Tomás once more. "Now then, me laddo, you and Don Alfonso here want me to take you to see the Mother. Well, as you say, that is my Purpose. So what day is it?"

Tomás had no idea what day it was and told the Bull so.

"Hmm," mused the Bull. "You see, if it's Tuesday, then I am out pawing. If it's Thursday, I am out snorting. Saturdays, as you may well imagine, are given over totally to charging up and down bellowing and creating all sorts of noise. Sunday, I have my hooves polished. Mondays are generally free, though."

"Do you know what day it is, sir?" Tomás asked.

"What was it yesterday?"

"I don't know," Tomás replied, but thinking quickly added, "What were you doing yesterday, sir?"

The Bull thought for a moment before replying.. "I was pounding up and down bellowing and creating noise yesterday. Perhaps you heard me?"

Tomás remembered the terrible thundering that

he and Don Alfonso had heard the evening before, and assumed that this had indeed been the Bull. "Then, yesterday was Saturday, so today is Sunday. So," he concluded confidently, "tomorrow is Monday, and you are free."

The Bull pawed the ground once more and shook his head. "Just a nonce, old thing, just a cotton pickin' moment. All this assumes that today is Sunday."

"But Sunday always follows Saturday. At least it does where I come from," Tomás smirked.

"Well, me laddo, you aren't where you come from. You are where I come from, and things are different. Besides, why should Sunday follow Saturday anyway?"

Tomás had to admit that he had no idea. All he knew was that Sunday followed Saturday and came before Monday, and always had.

Sensing the boy's doubt, the Bull continued, "What then, my young friend, would be wrong with today being Thursday, if we all wanted it to be?"

"Or Monday?" Don Alfonso offered helpfully.

"Or Monday," the Bull agreed.

"What is the point of having names for the days of the week if you don't keep them in order?" Tomás asked, a little testily.

The Bull shrugged his massive shoulders. "Does there have to be a point?" he asked.

"Of course there has," Tomás snapped.

"Why?"

"I don't know why. Only there has to be."

The Bull shook his massive head again and smiled. "We have so few humans along this way you know, and I can see why. Young man, listen to me, and listen carefully. What you see, and what you believe you see, are not always the same. How do you judge things; good, bad, sweet, sour, and so on? None of these things are anything other than ideas that you have about things."

Tomás shook his head. "I don't understand," he said.

The Bull adopted a more kindly tone. "Look here, my dear fellow," he said, "does the Moon, for example, count how many times she rises and sets? Of course she doesn't. Do mountains count the passing seasons? Why should they? Tomás, all time is simply the distance between two events. It is not important so, if we decide to do something tomorrow, then that marks out tomorrow from today."

Tomás agreed that it did.

"So," the Bull continued, "if we decide to go to the Mother tomorrow then we can call tomorrow what we like, can't we?"

Tomás agreed that they could.

"Now, when the sun rises tomorrow I shall take you to see the Mother."

"And call tomorrow Monday if we choose?" Don Alfonso suggested.

The Bull snorted enthusiastically. "What a capital idea!" he bellowed. "Now, if you gentlemen will excuse me, I have a hard day's snorting ahead of me. I do hope that you will make yourselves comfortable in my humble cave until I return."

"I'm sure that we shall," Don Alfonso assured him.

"In that case, gentlemen, I shall bid you 'Adios' for now," and with that, the Red Bull of Bailén ambled off snorting furiously to the left and right, creating great clouds of red dust that rose on either side of him as he went on his way.

Tomás sat down on a large rock at the mouth of the cave and scratched his head as he watched the Red Bull snorting off into the distance. "Well, he's not what I expected at all," he admitted. "I expected him to be fiercer, I don't know ... more like a Bull."

Don Alfonso curled up, contemplating a pleasant snooze. He yawned. "I suppose that is because you humans treat bulls so badly that they are bound to be fierce. I expect you would be too if they put you in a ring and threw spears at you, and then called it *sport*. For my part, I have always found bulls to be the most sophisticated and educated members of the animal kingdom, and the Red Bull is more so than most."

"You told me he was fierce," Tomás said accusingly.

Don Alfonso shook his head. "No, Tomás, I have

never told you that the Red Bull was fierce. You assumed that he was. It would have done no good though to tell you that you could never hope to meet a more civilized bull because, being a human person, you wouldn't have believed me." So saying, he curled up and went to sleep leaving Tomás to contemplate his meeting with the amazing Red Bull of Bailén.

As he thought about it, Tomás was amazed by just how much he had changed since he had begun the journey. What he had considered to be facts were, in reality, only assumptions, and assumptions, for it doesn't matter how many people believe them, were still only assumptions. This, the boy decided, was the big failing of people. He could understand now why Don Alfonso was always telling him to accept what *is* and not to ask questions all the time. People were people, dogs were dogs, and bulls were certainly bulls, but all had intelligence and feelings, and all had a Purpose and were linked together in the great web of being and doing. He could see now that if one thing ceased to be, then everything would cease to be, because the web that binds us all together would unravel and would cease to be too!

These thoughts spun round and round in his head until Tomás became quite dizzy from thinking about them. As he watched the day pass, he felt somehow differently about himself. He felt more content, more forgiving because he could see that everything was important. Though he couldn't explain it, Tomás knew he had completed a journey within himself, and now felt ready to go on.

That evening the Red Bull returned, still snorting up huge red clouds of dust. "A most satisfactory day's snorting," he announced, as he lay down, massively, in the cave mouth.

"Is that all you've done, Bull?" Tomás asked.

"Hard work it is too young man. Can't see your hoof in front of your horn in all that dust."

Tomás was about to ask what the point of all the snorting was, but checked himself for he realized now that it is very ignorant to judge what other creatures do based upon your own small experience. "I can imagine," he conceded.

Don Alfonso yawned and stretched himself. "Tell us something about the Mother, Bull old man, if you don't mind. We would hate to turn up and not know anything about her," he added.

The Red Bull thought for a moment before replying, "Funny you should mention that, old chap, but you're the second fellow to ask me about the old Madre."

"Who was the first?" Tomás asked eagerly.

The Bull bellowed with laughter. "Couldn't see, old man, couldn't see. Too busy snorting and raising dust, don'tcha know. Now the Madre, nice old stick I've heard, (never actually seen her meself), she lives on top of a mountain ages from here, and guards the Book," he added, more seriously.

"The Law of the Learned Pibroch Rat?" Tomás suggested.

"The very same, young feller me lad, the very same. She is very wise, should be too, the length of time she's been about. Guards the Book, as I say, and records the names of all creatures like you who walk to the Moon. By Jove what a woman!

"Now then, if you gentlemen will excuse me, I must eat. We bulls have to have our quota, don'tcha know, and we've got a long way to go tomorrow." So saying, he rose slowly to his huge brass-clad feet and, with a swish of his massive tail, began to eat slowly from a mountain of coarse grass that lay stacked in one corner of the cave.

The following morning the weather broke. Instead of the sun rising from behind the ragged peaks, the dawn appeared over the sierras beneath a huge mass of black cloud. Then, with little warning, save for a blast of cold, wet wind, there came a sudden streak of lightning that lit up even the very depths of the Red Bull's cavern. Moments later a grumbling, rumbling peal of thunder rolled across the plain, followed by another shaft of forked lightning and yet more deep thunder. Don Alfonso howled and tried to bury himself in the Red Bull's hay pile, leaving only the tip of his tail showing as he did so.

Slowly at first, so slowly that Tomás could count them, great raindrops began to fall, slapping loudly against the earth making the dust jump. Gradually the rain became faster and heavier as the storm moved over the mountains, until it was impossible to look out of the cave at anything but a thick curtain of falling water.

The Red Bull put his nose outside and sniffed the air. "Rain at last," he mused. "Just in time too, I'll be bound."

"It doesn't worry you?" Tomás queried.

The Bull laughed. "Not a bit of it, young feller me lad, not a bit. In fact it is the best thing that could have happened because the rain makes the grass grow, and green, growing grass is grazing for bulls. Not a bad line that, don'tcha think? Hmm, rain makes the grass grow, and green, growing grass is grazing for bulls. Yes, it has a ring to it!"

"When shall we set off for the Mother's, Bull?" Tomás asked tentatively, trying to disguise his impatience.

"Well, we can't go in this or we shall all have a jolly good soaking," the Bull replied.

Tomás was finding his impatience ever more difficult to control. "When will it stop?" he persisted.

The Bull laughed once more and shook his

mighty head. "My dear chap, such a thruster, such a thruster. The rain will stop when it wants to stop and not before. You see, Tomás, things happen because they are supposed to happen, not because we want them to do so."

"Don Alfonso says that," Tomás admitted.

"Well dogs, y'know, know a great deal."

"What do people know, Bull?" Tomás asked.

The Bull answered slowly. "People are a bit strange. Well, they are to me anyway. They seem to think that they know everything but, truth to tell, they know very little, but because they are vain and have forgotten the Law, that makes them very dangerous to the rest of us."

"How so?"

The Bull mused, "As I remember, the Official Eagle, that most official of birds, would not come near a scrap of a boy like you. The Polite Rats were worried too, as I recall."

Tomás was astounded by this information. "How do you know that?" he asked. "Has Don Alfonso been saying anything?"

"Calm down, young feller, calm down!" the Bull replied patiently. "I know because I know. We four-leggeds and the feathered folk have learned to fear people because we have learned not to trust them. You see, I trust Don Alfonso and he trusts me, and we both trust you, otherwise you wouldn't be here. But in general, people live in another way from us. We are as we are and can accept each other and the wonders of the natural world as they are, and not seek to change them. We live our lives in peace and one day, when we are ready in head and heart, we walk to the Moon."

"Will you walk to the Moon, Red Bull?"

The Bull tossed his head. "Oh yes, in some lifetime or another, probably," he replied airily.

"Do you think I am ready in head and heart, Red Bull?"

"Only you can know that, Tomás, old man," the Bull told him gently.

As they talked, so the storm passed over the highest peaks, and the thunder died to a distant rumble in the valleys far away. The rain gradually lifted until the black was almost entirely replaced by puffs of high white cloud and, for the first time that day, the sun shone down bright and warm. Only then did Don Alfonso emerge from beneath the haystack, and begin sniffing the cool, wet air from the cave's mouth.

"Well," the Red Bull announced, shaking his mighty body and making his muscles ripple, "the storm seems to have passed. So, we haven't much time to lose if I am to get you to the Mother on time. Tomás," he said briskly, "at the back of the cave you will find two large wicker baskets, a blanket and some harness. If you would be so kind as to bring everything here we shall be on our way in a jiffy."

As quickly as he could, Tomás did as he was asked. The Red Bull knelt down and explained to the boy how he should fix the harness. Willingly, and with some skill, for Tomás had helped the muleros many times at La Peña to harness their mules before they began their long day's journey, he laid the blanket over the Bull's massive spine so that the harness wouldn't rub, and attached the skeleton harness, drawing the girth strap just tight enough beneath the Bull's stomach. Next, he attached the two deep wicker baskets to large hooks on either side of the harness and half filled them with dry straw. The Bull stood up and walked up and down to check the fitting.

"Capital, capital!" he said. "Most comfortable. Now if you put dear old Don Alfonso into one of the baskets, you can scramble into the other, then we'll be on our way."

Chapter Ten

Drawbridge to the Moon

So, crouching in wicker baskets on the flanks of
the Red Bull of Bailén, Tomás and Don Alfonso
began their journey to the home of the Mother of
All who lived alone on top of the world and
watched out for the well-being of all her creatures.

What a journey it was too! On the back of the
Red Bull they thundered across the watery plains
of rainswept Spain, over passes in the wildest of
the wild sierras, where only scrub and lavender
grew and thin trees turned their seasoned shoulders to the sharp wind that howled down the
slopes.

Autumn turned to winter and onward they
pounded through country that became wilder and
rockier by the day until, at last, the Red Bull of
Bailén pulled up at the foot of a single, magnificent peak that towered high above the surrounding mountain ranges.

The Red Bull tossed his head and shook his
sweating flanks. "Here we are then, chaps," he

announced. "Can't stay, pressing business, what! Besides, too jolly cold in these parts for me. Give me the warm south anytime. Beats me why the old girl can't live somewhere warm and sunny. Make my job a whole lot easier."

"Where are we?" Tomás asked between chattering teeth. Never before had he been in a wilder, darker spot than this, and never had he felt colder.

"This, young feller me lad, is the peak known far and wide as 'La Madre de Todos,' the Mother of All, and the last and most dangerous part of your journey. From here, you must climb to the very top of La Madre where herself will be waiting for you."

Tomás pointed to the great wall of sheer rock that stretched upwards in front of them. "You must be joking!" he cried.

"You have no other choice," Bull replied.

"But we can't climb up there, it's impossible!" Tomás waved his arm frantically at the slippery rock face that disappeared into the grey of a darkening winter sky.

"Tomás, you have forgotten all that I told you," the Bull said, shouting to be heard over the howling wind that had sprung up since they arrived. "You can only walk to the Moon if your head and heart are ready. Your head has taken you thus far, now you must trust in your heart.

"Do not fear, my friends," he continued reassuringly, "simply climb. The Mother will guide you."

"It is growing dark, Bull," Tomás said fearfully.

"Climb, my little friend, just climb and you will make it. I know you will." The great Red Bull of Bailén turned and with a ringing 'Adios!' that echoed through that stormy waste, he thundered off without another word, snorting and blowing fearsomely as he went.

"What shall we do now?" Tomás asked, once the Bull was out of sight.

Don Alfonso, who had remained silent since they arrived shrugged his shoulders and started hobbling off towards the rock face. "I really don't see that we have much choice. We either climb or freeze to death down here," he observed, in his matter of fact way.

They began their climb with night falling fast. It was raining steadily now, but as they climbed so each foot hold was firm and though neither could see, it was as if their feet were being directed. The night grew colder and darker, and the wind howled mournfully around the high peaks. Up and up they climbed. The way, by this time, was becoming very difficult and painful for Don Alfonso. Each step he took was, in reality, a little painful leap that left him exhausted the higher that they climbed.

Then finally, he could go no further. Don Alfonso stopped and, gasping, admitted softly, "You must leave me, Tomás. I cannot go on, I'm afraid. It's this leg of mine, you see. It is just too far for me."

Tomás could just see his friend below him in the dark. "I'm not going to leave you now, Don Alfonso," he said firmly. "You got us into this and you don't get out of it that easily!"

Don Alfonso howled. "You people are all the same, you think that you know best. I'm telling you, Tomás, I cannot go another step."

The boy said no more but scrambled down to where his friend lay panting, and picked him up. To his surprise, Don Alfonso seemed much lighter than he remembered. Tomás did not give it another thought and, with the icy rain lashing his face and the cold pinching at his ribs, he carried his friend up into the night.

It was a cold, grey but dry dawn that found Tomás and Don Alfonso climbing just below the snowline. Carefully putting Don Alfonso down, Tomás looked back and was astonished at the slope up which they had climbed during the night. As the cloud cleared away, so a sheer drop fell away below them. It was impossible that anyone could have climbed such a mountain, and at night in driving rain too.

"How do you feel?" he asked, returning to Don Alfonso's side.

His friend looked up, his huge brown eyes sparkling in the morning light. "A bit stiff, tired, confused, but grateful to you, Tomás. Without you I would certainly not have made it."

Tomás laughed. "Just returning the favour," he said. "Or have you forgotten the Great Subterranean Lake and the Mighty Centre?"

Don Alfonso shook himself and stood up. "Can't be very far now," he said and limped off stiffly in the direction of the peak.

Now they both felt as if they were being hauled towards that peak by a very strong rope. Closer and closer they came to the top, until they reached a little valley just below the actual summit, where they stopped once more. There, in the full light of day they looked out over the plains towards the hazy shapes of the distant sierras. The air up here was cold and clear. Though he was both cold and wet, Tomás could feel neither; glowing as he was from the climb and filled with anticipation. "Now, where do we go from here?" he asked.

Don Alfonso ordered him to rest while he carried on a little way to investigate. Without further ado, his head erect, Don Alfonso hobbled off through the snow and disappeared over the ridge ahead.

He had only been gone a short while when he returned panting out the good news excitedly: "Tomás, we've made it! I've seen the smoke from a fire down in a forest just beyond the summit. It can only be the Mother. Come and see for yourself."

Tomás was up in an instant and, following close on Don Alfonso's heels, came to a little ledge some distance away where, sure enough, he could see a thin spiral of smoke rising from deep within a pine forest further down the slope. Slowly, carefully, they made their way down through the snow until they came to the dark, silent forest that seemed ready to swallow them up. Fearfully, the friends entered the darkness and were very soon lost amongst the trees, their footfalls cushioned by the soft carpet of sweetly smelling needles upon which they walked. Deeper and deeper they went, and the forest became darker and more silent. Tomás was sure that he was lost, but something, somewhere was guiding his feet with uncanny certainty.

They walked and walked for what seemed like an eternity until, at last, they came to a clearing, in which there stood a small hut made of pine logs with tiny green windows on each wall, a red door at the front and a crooked stone chimney from which a twist of smoke rose up into the cold winter's sky.

Tiredness and hunger overcame their fears more than anything else, and drove them towards that little red door which opened slowly, as if by magic, allowing them to enter.

Inside, on a strangely carved rocking chair beside a jolly fire, sat a hunched figure who was busily stirring a large pot that swung from a trivet over the blaze. As their eyes became accustomed to the darkness, they could see a heavy table of dark, carved wood, upon which lay a huge, leather-bound book.

"Come in, my dears," the hunched figure said, without turning from the pot she was stirring.

Cautiously Tomás led the way into the room. "Are you the Mother?" he asked nervously.

"Some call me that, Tomás,"" the figure replied.

Tomás was astonished that the Mother knew who he was. "How do you know my name?" he asked.

The Mother chuckled. "I know, Tomás, because I know. Now you and Don Alfonso come over here, and have some of this soup that I have made for you. You have both come a long way and I am sure that you are both tired and hungry."

Don Alfonso needed no second bidding and was very soon curled up in front of the roaring fire. The Mother poured out a bowl of soup which she set to one side to cool for the dog and then offered another piping hot bowl to Tomás who gratefully took it and started to eat. The soup was delicious and, as he sat by the blazing fire, he felt very happy.

As he ate, Tomás was able to watch the Mother as she carefully stirred herbs into her bubbling pot. He had carried with him an idea of how he thought that she should look, and had expected someone rather more spectacular than this

143

wizened little figure in the long green skirt, whose thick grey hair shimmered like silver in the half light of the room. But it was her eyes, bright and piercing like an eagle's, and her peace that overwhelmed him. For as he watched, Tomás felt that he had found the Mother he had never known, the Mother whose love was all-seeing and all-knowing.

"You are very quiet for a boy, Tomás," the Mother smiled softly as she spoke. "In my experience boys can rarely sit still for a long time."

Tomás was embarrassed for he knew he had been unable to look away and thought that the Mother would be angry with him.

"You and Don Alfonso have learned a good deal during your journey — not just about the world but, more importantly, about yourselves," the Mother said, laying aside her ladle and sitting back in her chair. "This is why you have made this journey, and why it will soon be over."

Tomás shook his head. "I'm afraid that I don't understand any of this, Mother. I wouldn't be here without Don Alfonso. It was he who found me and made me come on this journey."

"Can you read?" Mother asked, rising stiffly from the chair. She walked slowly across the room to the carved desk and the heavy book that lay upon it, beckoning Tomás to follow her.

"Not very well," he replied. Tomás had learned

144

to read at the orphanage, but had mostly forgotten how.

"No matter," Mother told him. "Just open up the Great Book for me."

Tomás did as he was told. The first page was covered in strange, coloured symbols that were interlinked in a series of patterns that appeared to move, changing shape and colour before his eyes. There were snakes, brilliantly coloured snakes that squirmed and intertwined along the border, slithering one into the other. Carefully, he turned the page to reveal these words written in large letters of gold:

> *Herewith Follows*
> *The Law*
> *According to the Most*
> *Noble &*
> *Learned*
> *Pibroch Rat.*

So, here it was, the Law of the Learned Pibroch Rat that he had heard so much about. "Is this the book?" Tomás asked, awestruck by what he was looking at.

The Mother laughed. "As far as I am aware Tomás, there are certainly not two of these Great Books."

Gently, Tomás drew his finger over the raised gold letters.

"Turn the page, Tomás."

The boy did as he was told and before his eyes the writing on the page dissolved and he saw himself sitting on the slopes of the Sierra Nevada, watching over Fat Francisco's goats. Then, from the top of the page Don Alfonso came hobbling towards him.

"This is you as you were, Tomás," the soft voice of the Mother commented. "Turn the pages and watch yourself develop."

As he did so, Tomás followed his journey with Don Alfonso. There was the Lady of the Snows on her crystal throne; next, the Wild Weaver of the Alpujarras. There were the Polite Rats ferrying them across the Great Subterranean Lake, and there, the fearsome Nunnapooses. The more pages that he turned, the more Tomás saw that the journey had not simply been a series of tests, but a journey of discovery — the discovery of himself!

When finally he reached the page where he and Don Alfonso arrived at the Mother's hut, Tomás experienced the strange sensation of being drawn into the book and, much to his surprise, found himself back on his chair, with a full bowl of soup in his hands. Don Alfonso was curled up on the floor and the Mother was sitting over the fire stirring herbs into her pot. It was the same, but somehow different. Since he could remember reading the Book he knew that everything he had experienced was real.

"Was I dreaming, Mother?" he asked.

"No child, you weren't dreaming. You finally came home."

"But where is this home, Mother?" he asked, more frightened than confused.

The Mother laughed. "Let's wake up Don Alfonso so that he can have his soup, then I shall tell both of you."

When Don Alfonso had finished his soup and was curled up in front of the fire at the Mother's feet, she began: "When you started this journey you never considered for a moment who you were. Now that you have almost finished your journey, you are sure of who you are: you now know *yourselves!*

"During your travels, without your knowing it, all the pretending, all the acting, all the great flummery that creatures build up about themselves in order to make themselves more acceptable to others, has gone, and a great weight has been lifted from you. Do you not feel it? It has been so slow, like a change in the seasons, that you haven't noticed it. But it has happened.

"You are ready to complete your journey to the Moon. She is waiting for you soon. In a day or two she will rise, framed by the two great standing stones between which the River of the Winter Season flows. I shall lead you to a place where you can watch the Moon rise, and when her face is clear of the river she will let her drawbridge down. At that moment, you must gather all your courage to you and step out on to the river. But be warned, a moment too soon or a moment too late and you will be swept away and lost forever. You must step fearlessly on to the drawbridge and walk towards the Moon without ever looking backwards. Do you understand?"

Both Tomás and Don Alfonso said they did, but both felt a twinge of fear and sadness that one last test lay before them. The journey so far had been like the title page of the Great Book, occupying neither space nor time, but this last test was to be the point of it all.

"Now you must sleep," the Mother ordered, "for I have many things to prepare before you go. Go to sleep."

Tomás had no idea how long he had slept, but he woke to find himself lying on a little bed of straw in the corner of the Mother's hut. Out of one eye he could see Don Alfonso and the Mother deep in conversation. He sat up with a start, for he sensed that something of importance was being discussed.

The Mother looked round and smiled gently. "Good," she said softly, "you are awake now. You have much to do."

Tomás shook the last of the sleep from his head and asked, in alarm, "What is it? What's happening?"

Mother beckoned him to the fire where he sat

down in a chair next to her. "Tomás," she told him seriously, "tonight is the night that you will walk to the Moon."

"Tonight?" the boy repeated softly. There was a certain finality about it all, now that there was no turning back. His stomach churned at the thought.

"Come, hold my hands, Tomás, and I shall tell you what I have just told Don Alfonso," the Mother said, taking hold of Tomás' hands in hers. They felt so soft and gentle that all thoughts of fear fled before that simple touch. "Tonight the Moon will be full and the air still. I will walk with you down to the River of the Winter Season, that flows at the foot of this mountain. As I told you when you arrived, you must wait until the Moon rises between the two pillars of rock that stand on either bank of the river. As the Moon continues to rise, there will come a time when it appears as if the river itself is pouring into the Moon. It is then that the river turns yellow in the moonlight, and it is at that precise moment that you must put your trust in the Moon and step out on to the river, and start to walk towards her."

"Walk on the river?" Tomás asked in astonishment.

"On this winter's night, and no other, the full Moon lets down her drawbridge for those creatures that seek her, and tonight is that night."

Tomás and Don Alfonso passed the rest of the

day helping the Mother to gather wood and clean her home until, at last, the shadows began to lengthen and they made ready for their final adventure.

In the gathering dusk, the Mother led Tomás and Don Alfonso down through the pine trees. The night grew darker as they left the trees and walked out on to a rocky stretch of open ground that ran down to a broad, swiftly flowing river, that surged and twisted noisily in the darkness beyond them.

"I will leave you here," the Mother told them. "If you look downstream you will see the two pillars of which I spoke."

Sure enough, they could see two gigantic pillars of rock rising blackly against the night, their peaks glinting white with the first dusting of snow.

"You must watch carefully," the Mother told them finally. "Your very lives will depend upon it. You will see the Moon rise perfectly between those two peaks. At the moment when her drawbridge comes down you must step out on to the road that will be created for you. You have no need of me now, my children. You belong to the Moon." Then, mysteriously, she was gone.

Tomás sat down on a rock and gazed downstream towards the peaks. Don Alfonso lay fearfully beside him. They had, at last, reached their goal ... almost. Tomás thought back to Granada — how long ago that seemed now! — with its fine churches, ornate houses and old Moorish palaces that floated magically below the majestic Sierra Nevada. Absently he wondered what Fat Francisco and Carmen were doing now. Who was looking after the goats? None of that mattered now. He felt a little pang of regret, homesickness, and a deeper fear of leaving all that was familiar to him. As he thought, a tear welled up in his eye and rolled slowly down his cheek.

Don Alfonso, too, was silent. He lay, as dogs sometimes do, with his head on his front paws and an empty look in his eyes. He was thinking of the happy nights he had spent in the company of Gabri, little Porro and all the other sheepdogs, as they sat round the campfire while the shepherd slept.

They were both lost in their thoughts, when they felt a presence nearby. Tomás leapt to his feet for there, to his utter astonishment, stood the largest, whitest sheepdog he had ever seen.

Don Alfonso struggled to his feet, calling out joyfully: "Gabri, why Gabri, my old friend. What on earth are you doing here?"

Gabri sat down wearily. "Well," he said, "I couldn't let you come all this way by yourselves now, could I?"

"You mean that you have followed us?" Tomás asked.

Gabri scratched himself. "I am an old dog now, Tomás. I have seen many things in my wanderings, and the Mother herself suggested I made this final trip.

"You see, Don Alfonso here has been a great support to me these last few years, so I offered him the chance to come too, but, as you know, he has a problem with his leg and needed to find someone to help him. So, I told him to begin by finding this someone, which was something that he had to accomplish himself if it was his Purpose to walk to the Moon. I discreetly followed to make sure that you both made it, and by following you and helping you out I was able to keep you out of trouble."

Tomás shook his head in disbelief, but said nothing. He had been right all along. They had been followed! But how had Gabri been able to help? He remembered the voices that he had heard at crucial moments during the journey, and the ball of string that saved them from the Nunnapooses. That had been Gabri, but how had he done it? Then he realized that none of that mattered now, only what lay ahead of them.

It was just as well, for as they spoke the Moon had steadily risen, and was now almost enclosed between the two great pillars. They waited and watched as the Moon rose higher and higher, until the whole, brilliant circle was almost clear of the water.

"Quickly!" Gabri urged, leading the way. "Let's go!"

Without caring or knowing where they ran, Tomás and Don Alfonso followed him down to the river bank where they could hear the raging water crashing over the jagged rocks, and feel the cold, damp wind of its passing. In an instant it all changed. A strange silence fell and the river that had, moments before, been thundering through the night ceased and suddenly began to congeal in the moonlight, turning a pale shade of yellow as it did so.

"Now!" Gabri commanded, jumping on to the water's surface. Don Alfonso scrambled blindly after him, but Tomás held back momentarily. It was as if strands of his past life were clinging to him, trying even at this late stage to hold him back.

"Tomás, be quick, JUMP!" the two dogs cried from the centre of the river.

Tomás closed his eyes tightly, his mind became a blank and he jumped, as if into nothingness — and landed with a heavy thud between Gabri and Don Alfonso.

"Shall we go?" Don Alfonso offered cheerfully as the boy clambered to his feet.

"After you," Tomás replied, smiling broadly.

Like three friends out for a Sunday afternoon stroll, the boy and the dogs set off along the river between the two snowcapped pillars, and onwards to the Moon who shone softly, lighting their way.

Afterword

A few nights ago, a beautiful and clear full moon rose into the cloudless night sky. There was an early dusting of snow on the highest peaks of the Sierra Almijara making them float like ghosts in the moonlight. At that moment, I thought of my friend, Gabri, the wisest and daftest dog I had ever known. Don Alfonso's daughter, Titch, sat beside me and we watched, wondering if any creatures were walking to the Moon that very night.

Spain is a magical country, full of mystery and wild tales. Old Pepe, a man from our village who lived for all but eight years of the past century, told me some of the most wonderful stories that I have ever heard — tales of kings and queens; of bandits and lost villages; and of the Moorish people who for centuries worked the land that I now work.

It was Pepe who told me of the Lady of the Snows, and of the little gypsy folk, the Gitanillos. He also told me of the wild flowers, and of the birds and animals that thrive in the pure upland air.

Pepe has gone now, but when I look up towards

those wild, grey peaks I can sometimes see him walking there in the company of all those characters that he knew so well.

Without Pepe and Gabri I would never have been able to pass on this little tale to you. And that, I suppose, is my Purpose.

Nicholas Cross

Malu's Wolf

Ruth Craig

Malu's cave-dwelling clan lives according to the Animal Master's laws, and yet no animal has ever lived among them. So, when Malu rescues Kono, an orphaned wolf cub, the clan's wise man issues a stern decree: if Kono ever harms one of the clan she must die.

Defying the clan's taboos, Malu secretly learns to hunt while teaching Kono to follow her and live in harmony with the other cave-dwellers.

The wolf is gradually accepted by the clan but there are still some who want Malu dishonoured and Kono dead, and eventually Malu must choose between her wolf and her clan.

Malu's Wolf is a beautiful depiction of the taboos and harsh realities experienced by our pre-historic ancestors, and their reliance on the natural world to provide their means of survival.

Flyways

Five Days of the Ghost

William Bell

Exploring a sacred Indian burial ground in the middle of the night isn't Karen's idea of a great start to the holidays. But she lets her brother, John, talk her into it and that night they row across the lake to the forbidden island.

What they find there plunges them into a world they never thought existed — a world where past and present blend and the spirits of the dead communicate with the living.

With the help of John's schoolfriend, Weird Noah, an expert on the supernatural, Karen and John try to unravel the mystery that suddenly invades their lives and fills their home with strange happenings.

Fascinated and afraid, Karen is forced to confront the tragic events in her life that she has refused to face up to now.

Flyways